Onions and Oranges

A Willis Prescott Mystery

Kathy Dorsey

Published by Freiling Agency, LLC.

P.O. Box 1264
Warrenton, VA 20188

www.FreilingAgency.com

PB ISBN: 978-1-963701-98-2
E-book ISBN: 978-1-963701-14-2

Dedicated to:

Family and Friends

"I would not wish
Any companion in the world but you."

William Shakespeare, *The Tempest,* Act III, Scene I

1

USPS Receipt
840-5320-0239-001-00031-46706-01

As I stand in the Fountain Square branch of the Citrus Heights post office, I wonder why the line in front of me is so long. It's a Thursday morning in the middle of September. To the best of my knowledge, September 16 has no special significance. So what is it about today that has so many people at the post office? I look around for clues. Because some people have parcels, I know they need special attention. The postal clerk has to weigh each one and enter each delivery address into the computer. Even though these procedures are supposed to be computerized, they take more time than they should. Amazon processes orders in seconds and delivers in a day. I wonder why can't our postal service perform in the same way. With every minute that passes, the line gets longer.

Many customers in line ask for stamps. Each time, in response, the postal clerk asks what kind of stamps they want. Some say they like the stamps with pictures of flags, while others say they like the stamps with pictures of flowers. I don't understand why pictures on stamps are important to the buyers. After all, a sender doesn't receive the envelope with the cancelled stamp, the addressee receives it. Except for stamp collectors, how many people look at the stamp when they receive an envelope? All these postal decisions and transactions take time. With every minute that passes, the line gets longer as my patience gets shorter. At least, the long line is now behind me rather than ahead of me.

You may wonder why I am in line at the post office rather than in my chair at my office. Today, my need is different from the others in front of me. I don't have a parcel, and stamps aren't on my list. Instead, I need to have my envelope "certified." I have already filled out the green postal form in order to help save time with the postal clerk. Nonetheless, the procedure will still take time. I wish I could avoid it. If my client had paid her balance on time, I could have, but she didn't. So, here I am with my envelope that contains my third and final notice. Once it's certified, mailed, and the green postal card is returned to me, I will know for certain if it has been received by the person to whom my envelope is addressed. This step and receipt of final payment will complete an investigation that started about nine months ago.

I was surprised when Mrs. McIntyre failed to pay her last installment for my investigative services. In the past, she either handed me a check or mailed one within a few days of receipt of my invoices. Until now, she never let me down. Then, of course, I provided her information she wanted to hear. At the end of my assignment, I told her some information she couldn't bear to hear, which I suspect now accounts for her payment delinquency. But I can't afford to let sentiments get in the way of my business. I completed a service for Mrs. McIntyre, and now, I expect her to pay this final invoice.

Clients often retain me to find their deadbeat accounts. Because I know where Mrs. McIntyre lives, I don't need to trace her, but I do need to hold her to account. Mrs.

McIntyre retained me. She signed a contract for my services. I took her case when law enforcement told me it was a waste of time. I did my job, and I did it well. Whether she likes it or not, I can't help how her case turned out. Facts are facts.

As a private investigator and as a former police officer, I know life throws us curves. No matter how rich or poor, all lives are complex. When I take on a case, I don't have to look far to find joy or sorrow in equal measures, plus a whole range of emotions in between. When I solve a case, I can be as surprised by the outcome as any of my clients. Mrs. McIntyre's case was one of those that produced unexpected results. She was surprised by what I found. Like her, I was surprised too. What I found out made Mrs. McIntyre unhappy. Unlike her, it didn't make me unhappy, but then, James McIntyre wasn't my son, either. Let me explain.

2

File No. 16-12-07MCI

I received my first telephone call from Mrs. McIntyre on December 7, 2016. For many, December 7 is an important date because it marks the anniversary of Pearl Harbor and our entry into the Second World War. Until 2016, though, December 7 held no special significance for me. It was a day like any other day. None of my family served in that war or any other, as far as I know. But Lorna McIntyre's call changed December 7 for me. It's a date that now lives in infamy for Mrs. McIntyre and for me.

I had just arrived at my office, pulled out my chair from behind my desk, and set my coffee down when the telephone rang. Before the third ring, I picked up the receiver. "Good morning. Prescott Investigative Services. Willis Prescott here. How may I help you?"

The line was open, but no one spoke. I wondered if this was another one of those pesky robotic telephone calls. Should I hang on and wait until someone tried to sell me something or should I hang up? I hung on. Several more seconds elapsed before I heard a woman's voice say, "Mr Prescott?"

"Yes, this is he. How may I help you?"

Another few seconds passed without any response, and I said, "Hello, is there someone there?"

Nothing. Although this additional delay frustrated me, it also piqued my curiosity. Who was on the other end of the line and what was behind the reticence? Finally, the woman spoke again. This time, in one breath, she let out a stream of sentences.

"My name is Lorna McIntyre. I was referred to you by Mike White. He said you could help me. It's about my son. The police called it an accident. It wasn't. They closed the case. My son was murdered. I need you to help me find my son's killer. I can pay. When can we meet?"

Lorna McIntyre was breathless when she finished and sounded exhausted. As she gasped for air, I drew in a deep breath to buy time before I responded to her. Despite more than thirty years' experience, I could not remember a call like Lorna McIntyre's, and I have a good memory. My ability to recall details is what made me a good police detective and now makes me an equally good private investigator. Why did Mike White refer this woman to me?.

Mike and I are best friends. We worked together throughout our twenty-five years for the Sacramento Police Department. Since I left SPD, we have stayed in touch and meet for drinks every couple of months. Mike is a great cop and a great guy. If the police closed this case, why would he refer this woman to me? Perhaps this was Mike's idea of a prank. Was this his attempt at getting even for all the jokes I played on him? No, I knew better. After thirty-seven years, you get to know a guy. Mike doesn't play pranks on anyone. They aren't part of his M.O. As I sat and thought about this call, my reverie was broken by Mrs. McIntyre. "When can we meet?"

Because I didn't have much on my plate and the upcoming holidays meant a slowdown in my business anyway, I decided to meet with Lorna McIntyre. I was curious to meet the woman behind the voice. Why did she call me? Why did she believe her son was murdered? Why did the police close the case? And what did she look like? We set up an appointment for ten o'clock on December 10, and I agreed to meet with Mrs. McIntyre at her home.

I wondered what her home was like. Could she afford my services? I didn't have to wait long to find out answers to some of my questions. As soon as Mrs. McIntyre gave me her address, I knew she lived in an expensive part of Sacramento, so I knew she should be able to pay me.

In order to help, I explained to Mrs. McIntyre that I needed every bit of information she had about her son's case—no matter how small or incidental.

"So, Mr. Prescott, you'll help me?"

"I'll let you know after we meet on the tenth."

"The tenth at ten," she repeated and that was all Lorna McIntyre said before she hung up.

I pulled an empty beige folder out of my file cabinet drawer. On the blank tab in the upper left corner, I wrote 16-12-07MCI. My file system was a simple one. The first two digits stood for the year. The second two digits stood for the month. The third two digits stood for the day, and the last three letters stood for the first three letters of the company's name or, in the case of an individual, the client's surname. This file system works well for me. I've been in business for myself for more than ten years and I've never misplaced or lost a file. I admit I had cases I wanted to lose, but the files remained in the cabinet, regardless.

Before I put Lorna McIntyre's file in my cabinet, I jotted additional information on a pink sheet of paper. I use pink lined paper pads as intake forms because pink stands out in files that can become inches thick with paper. Papers can include copies of medical or accident reports, statements, photographs, receipts, and a host of other items pertinent to a case. Every piece of paper is important, although sometimes its importance is not apparent. Files full of paper can be difficult to wade through. A file can be cumbersome. So much paper can make it difficult to focus, too, especially if I have more than one case file on my desk at a time. As long as I can refer to that pink piece of paper, I can always get back on track.

During my telephone conversation with Lorna McIntyre, I had already penned some details, such as the date, time of her call, her name, telephone number, and address at the top of the page. Below these items, I compiled a list of additional comments with question marks after each. They were brief. To remind me later why I decided to meet with Mrs. McIntyre, I listed: "son?"; "Mike White?"; "accident?"; and "murder?"

I was tempted to call Mike White before I met with Lorna McIntyre but decided to wait. Any discussion with Mike was premature until I heard whatever Mrs. McIntyre had to tell me and reviewed whatever she had to give me. Yet, in the back of my mind, I knew that Mike referred Mrs. McIntyre to me for a reason. I had to find out what it was and why he gave her my name. Although I didn't need a pretext to call Mike, this was a good one. I planned to call him on December 11.

Meanwhile, I tore this pink sheet off the pad, punched two holes at the top, and affixed it to the double clasps at the top of the folder. Then I put the folder in my file cabinet where it would remain there for the next three days. On December 10, I would pull it from the file cabinet before I left my office to meet with Lorna McIntyre.

3

Badge No. 1919

I leaned back in my chair, lifted my legs, crossed them, and set my shoes on top of my desk. That day, I wore my brown tasseled loafers. Inside them, my feet were bare. They felt good. My shoes and feet were comfortable. No more black socks. For twenty-five years, I wore them just like all other law enforcement officers, even prison guards. I chuckled over this small indulgence. While I sipped my coffee, I reflected on Lorna McIntyre's call. It perplexed me. Where it would lead? The possibilities made my mind wander back to when I started on the police force, almost thirty-seven years ago.

When I became a police officer, I had no idea I would stay long enough to retire after twenty- five years. I also had no idea I would leave SPD to start a private investigation business. I joined the police force right out of high school. Many of my classmates went on to college, but four more years of school did not appeal to me. Unlike them, I wanted to start work right away and in a job that offered me a way to get ahead. As a boy, I always wanted to be a policeman, although my desire may have been based more on the allure of the uniform than of the job. I have always been a clothes horse.

I was eighteen when I applied at the City of Sacramento for a job with the police department. Just in case the police department didn't accept me, I also applied at the county for a job with the sheriff's department and at the state for a job with the California Highway Patrol. I liked the police department's navy blue uniform better than the sheriff's department's dark green one or the state's khaki one. I was grateful the city came through first. With my deep blue eyes and fair hair, I couldn't see myself in dark green or khaki, not to mention the wide-brimmed hats that sheriff deputies and highway patrol officers wore. Neither would frame my face like the peaked hat police officers wore. When I was eighteen, I believed clothes made the man, so I also believed the city police uniform would make me a better man and a better officer. In retrospect, those beliefs may seem silly, but at the time, they gave me the confidence I needed. When you're a teenage boy, confidence is often in short supply.

Before I could go to the police academy, I had to spend the first four months on routine tasks. Every day, I was assigned to an officer who had me do whatever he or she wanted me to do. Most had me tidy their desks and put their reports in some sort of order, which could vary by officer. Some liked their reports organized by date, while others liked them organized by incident. Some officers explained why I was asked to perform certain tasks, but most others just saw me as a file clerk, someone they expected to figure out what they wanted and fast. If I was lucky, they might ask me to go out and buy them coffee, and if I was luckier, they might chip in and buy me one too. Until then, my drink of choice was Dr. Pepper.

To this day, I can still remember how those officers liked their coffees. Some liked it regular; this meant with milk and sugar. Others liked it with milk only and no sugar, others liked it black with sugar only and no milk, and a few liked it black with no milk or sugar. The amount of milk and sugar each wanted could vary. The first few times I got coffees was a challenge. I screwed up a few of the orders. The officers weren't pleased and let me know it. But, by the end of my first week, I got the hang of it. No matter how they liked their coffees, after all these years, I still like mine black with two sugars. It's been a long time since I've enjoyed a Dr. Pepper.

Although I didn't have much time to linger over the officers' reports, as often as possible, I tried to read them in order to get a sense of what police work was all about. It didn't take long for me to learn that every incident to which an officer is called requires a report. The police department has a standard incident report format, which is several pages long and has many boxes to tick, data lines to complete, and room for additional information. Police record facts and only facts. Adjectives and adverbs are redundant in police reports.

Most incident reports are traffic related, and most involve drivers who exceed the speed limit or who fail to obey stop signs at intersections. The descriptive areas of these reports are brief compared to other types reports, but they do contain all pertinent particulars, such as date, time, place, and driver information. They have to contain a lot of detail because officers never know when they may face a driver in court. A police report may make the difference between a conviction and an acquittal. No police officer wants to go to court and lose a case because of an incomplete report. While such a loss may be good for the driver's record, it's not good for a police officer's record or opportunity for promotion.

Other traffic related incidents can be more serious, especially if cars collide or if a car hits a pedestrian. Reports for these incidents have more detail and are often accompanied by photographs of the accident scene. If the incident involves a fatality, others are involved, such as members of the forensic evidence team and the medical examiner's office. Each has to complete a report too. A serious traffic accident may happen in a matter of seconds but take hours to investigate, reconstruct, and record.

Beyond traffic reports, police encounter other types of incidents. Some involve crimes, such as burglaries or illegal drugs, while others may involve domestic disturbances or disputes. All require reports.

Early in my career, I discovered police officers devote large chunks of time to reports. If you can't find a cop when you need one, it's probably because of reports. I learned the downside of police work is that much of it is routine and involves reports; and I also learned the upside is that a lot of police work is routine and involves reports. I never failed to complete one and never lost a case in court, which may account for my rise through the ranks.

Of course, police work isn't just routine traffic stops and reports. It can be dangerous. After all, police deal with criminals. On any day, a police officer never knows what is around any corner. Each day brings new challenges. Most are easy to overcome, but others can put an officer at grave risk. Those risks are why police officers now wear bullet-proof vests. I was sorry when that day came. While I understood a bullet-proof vest could save my life, the vest meant I didn't look as good in my uniform. My uniform served as my ticket to dates with women and three marriages. A bullet-proof vest got in the way. It also reminded women that police work is dangerous while I tried to convince them that it wasn't.

After four months of grunt paperwork for officers, the city sent me to the police academy where I spent the next six months. It was tough. It was intensive. I learned a lot. I also met other officers who became life-long friends. Those twenty-six weeks gave me a solid foundation for the next twenty-five years and my best friend, Mike White.

My career and Mike's careers ran parallel, although I moved to the detective squad when Mike preferred to stay on the beat. He liked day-to-day interactions with people in the neighborhood. It allowed him to build relationships that he used later when he moved to anti-drug enforcement. We earned our promotions at about the same time. We both rose through the ranks and became lieutenants. Although we often found ourselves in the same precincts, we were never partners. Perhaps that's why we stayed such good friends.

When I retired to start my business, I asked Mike to join me. He refused. Instead, Mike stayed with Sacramento Police Department.

Mike always says "when I retire, I plan to turn in my badge and gun for a rod and a reel." That's Mike. No one likes to fish more than him. When he isn't with his wife and his kids, he is at the river. Mike never reveals if he's caught any fish. I don't think he cares. I asked him once why he liked to fish and what he liked to catch, and he just shrugged his shoulders and said, "When I fish, I connect with nature and I catch my thoughts."

Mike never did expand on his response. He didn't need to. Anyone who's met Mike finds him to be like I have always found him: placid—which, for a police officer, is uncharacteristic. Most police officers, like me, are edgy. Mike's time at the river works for him. I wish it would work for me. I tried to fish once but couldn't stand the solitude.

Despite our different temperaments, Mike and I have become, and remain, good buddies. Opposites attract. We did. Mike puts up with me.

During my policing days, when we'd hit the bars after work, Mike would sip his beer while I'd canvassed the room to look for my next date.

"Will, when will you settle so we can talk?" He'd always ask. "Just as soon as I find the right one," I'd say.

"And, you say you don't like to fish."

My standard response to Mike is always: "I like to catch and release." To this day, every time I say it, Mike laughs.

4

Mike White

Mike White proposed to his high school sweetheart just as soon as we graduated from the police academy. The ink wasn't dry on his diploma when he presented a diamond engagement ring to Tonya. For the next twelve months, they planned their big day, although I suspect Tonya may have been more involved than Mike.

I was flattered when Mike asked me to be his best man. Tonya's bridesmaids widened my field of prospective girl-friends. When they saw me in my tuxedo, I was sure they would find me hard to resist. I wanted to meet someone new. If I met a girl who was a friend of my friend, I hoped to have a better relationship. I didn't know a lot about women, but I did know that a guy never asked his girlfriend to accompany him to wedding unless he wanted to give her ideas about marriage. I had no interest in marriage, and I had no steady girlfriend either, so neither were problems.

Somehow, I must have mentioned to Mike how good I looked in a tuxedo. Most often, Mike either laughs or ignores me when I brag. His indifference doesn't stop me. This time, though, he paid attention.

"Will I need a tuxedo for our wedding? Will the grooms-men will need them too? Where do you go to get a tuxedo?"

For my junior and senior high school proms, I rented tuxedos from Harper and Hogan. It was an easy decision. I went to high school with Alex Harper, Junior. His father, Alex Harper Senior, owned the store, along with a man named John Hogan. Mr. Harper and Mr. Hogan had been in business together for as long as I could remember. Their store was a prominent Sacramento business. Not only was it attractive to look at, but the front windows always displayed clothes that I wished that I could afford to wear. The inside of the store was decorated in dark woods and thick plaid carpet. If you could afford to buy shoes, you sat on leather chairs while Mr. Harper or Mr. Hogan fitted you.

Alex Junior worked part time at Harper and Hogan after school every Thursday and Friday. He also worked all day on Saturdays. Of course, none of us called him Alex. We called him by his nickname, Luthor. He went from Alex to Lex, from Lex to Lex Luthor and from Lex Luthor to Luthor. Although his nickname made sense to his classmates, I don't think it made sense to anyone else. Alex's mother always said, "Who?" when we called his house and asked for Luthor.

Unlike comic book Luthor, nothing about Alex was villainous. He was a really nice guy and funny too. No one we knew was a better mimic than Alex. His impersonations of teachers and celebrities were as good as anyone you might see on television. Alex picked up and magnified idiosyncrasies most of us missed or took for granted. It's difficult to explain, but he didn't mimic anyone in a mean way. Teachers even laughed when they caught him in the act.

When Alex graduated high school, he went right to work at Harper and Hogan. He always said that was what he planned to do. Although he was a straight-A student, Alex had no desire to go to college. As he also said, "I have a ready-made job that I enjoy now. Why would I want to spend four years at college and come back to do the same job? The pay won't be any better." None of us, most particularly me, could argue with him.

It made me happy to introduce Mike White to Alex Harper. As I expected, Alex took Mike under his wing. He wasted no time and asked Mike what seemed to be hundreds of questions. Alex wanted to know if Mike wanted to rent or buy. Then, he wanted to know the date, the time of day, the color of the bridesmaids' dresses, the names of the church and reception hall, plus many other items that made me ask, "Why do you need to know all this stuff?"

Although I'm sure he didn't have to, Alex proved to Mike and me why he was the right choice for Mike's tuxedo. Alex explained that he wanted to be sure that Mike not only looked good on the most important day of his life but felt comfortable too. "I don't want to rent or sell you a tuxedo that will make you feel too hot if the church isn't air conditioned. Your tuxedo should also complement the style of the bridesmaids' dresses. Years later, when you look at your photographs, you'll want to see homogeneous images."

"Wow" was all Mike and I could say. Who knew that the guy with whom I once swapped sandwiches in the high school cafeteria knew so much about wedding attire.

Alex suggested that Mike bring in his fiancé for a consultation.

"I believe it's advisable for the bride to be an active participant in the selection process. Once the two of you know what type of tuxedos you prefer, then we can set up times for the groomsmen to come in at their convenience."

Mike made an appointment for himself and Tonya.

A few days later, Mike told me how impressed he was with Alex and thanked me. More importantly, he told me

Tonya was impressed. "She can hardly wait to meet Alex. Although I got to tell you, she was surprised you knew anyone so professional."

I knew then I had my work cut out for me. No matter how good I looked in a tuxedo, I had to do more to impress Tonya, and by extension, her bridesmaids if I planned on a new relationship with any one of them.

5

Sergeant Coughlin

During the next twelve months, while Mike and Tonya were busy with their wedding plans, I had nothing to do as their best man until about four weeks before their big day. Then, I had to make plans to host Mike's bachelor party. Like any best man, I wanted Mike's party to be one that he and everyone else who attended would never forget. His party had to be one that blew his black socks off. The problem was neither Mike nor I was twenty-one. Mike had three months to go before his twenty-first birthday, and I had fourteen months to go. Because I was below the legal age, I couldn't reserve a room in a licensed establishment to hold the party. If I could find an unlicensed place to hold the party, I wasn't old enough to buy the liquor to serve at it. No one would buy tickets to a bachelor party without booze. As a newly minted police officer, I wasn't about to use a forged birth certificate and jeopardize my career before it got started. What was I going to do? This party seemed to be doomed before it got off the ground.

Weeks and then another month went by, and plans for the bachelor party were non-existent. I worried and lost sleep. It never occurred to me to ask for help. When you're twenty, you believe that you can do it all. Fortunately, others knew better. About three and a half months before the wedding, Sergeant Coughlin approached me.

"A little bird told me that you're Mike White's best man. We think a lot of Mike. What have you got planned for his bachelor party?"

The look on my face must have given me away.

"I thought so. You're stuck aren't you, kid?"

In a rush of words that must have taken him by surprise, I explained the problem. Sergeant Coughlin threw back his head and howled with laughter.

"Why didn't you say something sooner? You young pups always think you have all the answers. Thank goodness we old dogs know better. Okay, here's what you do. Go down the street to Alf's Bar and Grill. I'll call and let him know you're on your way. Tell him when and what you want for the party. He'll give you a cost per head. Alf won't need a total until a few days before the event. Once you're through at Alf's place, come back and see Lieutenant Anderson over in the Vice Squad. He'll know how to find you a couple of strippers for the evening. If you're lucky, the strippers will owe the lieutenant a favor and you won't have to pay them. After you're through with Alf and Lieutenant Anderson, come and see me and we'll work out the finer details. And next time, remember where you work and how we work. You're part of a family here. We have no room for officers that don't get it. Understand, Prescott?"

In a matter of minutes, I understood better than anything I had ever understood in my life. Sergeant Coughlin came through for me in ways that I never imagined. I learned a valuable lesson and one that I needed to learn if I ever wanted to fit in. As a young pup, I also learned how much I still needed to learn if I ever wanted to become an old dog.

Sergeant Coughlin and I met every week until the day of the bachelor party. We developed a rapport that made me feel more and more comfortable in the department. Sergeant Coughlin was tough but wanted what I wanted: a great bachelor party that would not only knock Mike's socks off but would make others envious of our department's group spirit.

Leo Coughlin was a great teacher and would have made an equally great accountant. He taught me how to identify all the items for the party (plus any contingencies), arrange them on a spread sheet, and develop a budget from which we could figure out ticket cost. Sergeant Coughlin insisted that we tack on an additional ten dollars per ticket so we could give Mike enough money for his honeymoon. This would never have crossed my mind. Although he made it look easy to plan, the bachelor party was beyond my abilities. Yet, Sergeant Coughlin never made me feel stupid. Instead, he made me feel like I was an important member of his police family.

After the tickets were printed, Sergeant Coughlin helped me sell them. He enlisted Lieutenant Anderson to sell them too. Guys who turned me down didn't turn Sergeant Coughlin down. While his rank may have influenced them, I believe they bought tickets from Sergeant Coughlin because he earned their respect in the same way he earned mine. One day, I hoped that I would be worthy of that kind of respect.

6

Ticket No. 2

We printed 350 tickets for Mike White's bachelor party. Because Sergeant Coughlin did so much to make it a reality, I set aside ticket number one for him. I also set aside tickets number two and three. Ticket sales were easier than either Sergeant Coughlin and I thought. I addition to the other officers who bought them, Alex Harper called and asked for twenty tickets. He planned to buy one and attend the party. Alex also thought he could sell some to his customers.

"Why don't you call our classmates? I'm sure the guys would enjoy a bachelor party. Tell them, they can stop by the store and buy their tickets here."

My former classmates surprised me. Everyone I called was happy to buy a ticket and said that they couldn't wait to go to a real bachelor party. To a man, all asked, "Will there be strippers?" They made me wonder why I had spent so much time on the menu, which, by the way, was great. Alf suggested hot roast beef, rolls, barbeque beans, macaroni salad, coleslaw, corn on the cob, and all types of snacks, including potato chips, dips, and peanuts. Sergeant Coughlin told me not to bother with dessert.

"After a few drinks, none of those guys will care. And don't bother with any party decorations either. No one will notice. Don't spend any money on frivolous things. Guys don't need that kind of stuff."

I didn't have the heart to tell Sergeant Coughlin that thoughts of dessert or party decorations hadn't crossed my mind.

When I reminded Sergeant Coughlin that Alf's Bar and Grill capacity was two hundred and fifty people, he told me that not everyone who buys a ticket shows up. This was news to me.

"A lot of people like to show their support for police functions, so they buy tickets to our events. It makes them feel good. Some see tickets as a way to get in our good graces. If they're pulled over, they'll show the ticket with the hopes an officer will forego a citation. It never works, but on the other hand, we don't tell nor discourage them. As far as we're concerned, they can think whatever they like."

Although Mike's bachelor party was no surprise to him, he was surprised when he heard about the number of guys who planned to attend. Mike asked about tickets for his other groomsmen. He was afraid that they might miss out.

"Don't worry. Just give me their names and telephone numbers and I'll make sure they get their tickets."

Mike told me that his cousin Jerry and Tonya's two brothers, Johnny and Tony, were groomsmen. By the end of the day, I had reached all of them. They were pleased to learn about the party and promised to send their checks. We agreed it was time we met.

For Mike's bachelor party, we sold 346 tickets. Sergeant Coughlin was pleased.

"Don't worry about the last four, we'll probably sell them tonight at the door. Speaking of numbers, did you do as I told you? Did you give Alf the right number?"

By right number, Sergeant Coughlin meant 233. Even though we sold 346 tickets, Sergeant Coughlin told me to tell Alf to expect 233. Sergeant Coughlin didn't believe everyone would show up. But I didn't believe more than 100 would stay away either. In my opinion, the right number was closer to 300 than 200. I was worried we wouldn't have enough food for everyone and I relayed my concerns to Sergeant Coughlin.

"This is a big night for Mike and me. I don't want either of us to be embarrassed."

As always, Sergeant Coughlin brushed aside my concerns.

"Kid, it doesn't matter how many really show up. Alf's kitchen can cook and serve food faster than any of us can eat it. Alf has been in business for a long time. He knows how this game is played. Do you think he cares about the number of meals he's going to serve tonight? No. Alf cares about the amount of booze he's going to sell to all these guys. He'll make more money on beer and liquor sales than he'll ever make on meals. You don't need to worry. I'll see you at Alf's. Be there by seven so we can take care of any last minute details. Don't be late."

I could see Sergeant Coughlin shake his head from side to side, and I could hear him chuckle as he walked away from me.

I finished my shift and headed home. On the way, I decided to stop for a haircut, as I knew I wouldn't have time before the ceremony and reception the next day. Besides, I wanted to look good for the party.

After my shower, I shaved and dressed. I put on my best jeans and brown western boots. I picked out a shirt from the closet, did up the pearl buttons, and took a look at myself in the mirror. By any standards, I looked good. I knew I would look even better in my powder blue tuxedo.

I arrived at Alf's by six forty-five. As I locked my car, Sergeant Coughlin pulled in next to me.

We walked into Alf's together.

"Well, kid, tonight's the night. There's not much else we can do now except have a good time. Let me buy you a beer. I know you're not old enough for liquor, but beer ain't nothing like the hard stuff. It takes a whole lot of beer to have any affect. Just remember, don't drink and drive. And if this place gets raided, you're on your own."

Sergeant Coughlin laughed as he spoke, which lightened the mood and took away any last worries about the party. The thought of having beer that night had not crossed my mind. I expected to drink sodas along with Mike and my underage classmates.

Over the past few months, I had learned more about how to plan a party than I did about police work, but to me, that party was just as important as my career. At eight, guys started to arrive. At first, I recognized no one. Sergeant Coughlin seemed to know everyone. It wasn't long before the place was packed. I was delighted to see at least a dozen classmates to whom Alex had sold tickets. I was also surprised to see Alex's father and his business partner, Mr. Hogan. As Alex told me later, "They like to party as much as anyone else." He made me wish I had invited my dad too. However, I had no idea if my father liked to go to bachelor parties.

I didn't have the kind of relationship with my father that Alex had with his father. As long as I can remember, my father worked the afternoon shift at the Campbell's Soup plant. By the time I got home from school, he was on his way to work. By the time he got home from work, I was in bed. Except for the time my mother and I spent with him during his two-week vacation, I seldom saw my dad. I loved and liked him, but I didn't know him.

By ten, the party was in full swing. As I looked around the room, I could see everyone with drinks in their hands or plates of food. A sign of a good party is lots of laughter. I heard plenty of laughter and lots of guffaws, I thought, *so far so good.* Out of the corner of my eye, I saw Sergeant Coughlin signal for me to come over.

"It's time for you, as best man, to make a toast to Mike."

I didn't remember if Sergeant Coughlin and I ever discussed a toast. But it didn't matter. I had enough beer in me to believe that I could do or say anything.

Sergeant Coughlin and the officers around him tapped their glasses with forks. It was a sign for the room to be quiet. I stood up on a chair so everyone could see me. The crowd responded and yelled, "Speech! Speech!" The words did not come as easily as I hoped, but I managed to say some nice things about Mike and how I was honored to be his best man. I also thanked Sergeant Coughlin for his help. Because he was such a big help, I told the crowd he held ticket number one. Because Mike was the honoree, I told the crowd he held ticket number two, even though he was number one in my book. I thanked everyone else for their support, as well as Lieutenant Anderson. Because he arranged for the strippers, I told the crowd he held ticket number three. Then, I knew enough to ask everyone to raise their glasses and salute Mike White. As I jumped down from the chair, the crowd yelled, "Stripper! Stripper!" It was time for the real entertainment to begin. Ticket holder number three was now the most popular guy in the room.

Someone turned on music. It was nothing I had ever heard on the radio, but it seemed like something that might accompany a striptease. To my right, I saw a couple of women come into the hall. They were dressed in the gaudiest red outfits I had ever seem. Around their necks, they had feathered scarves that they twirled in front of them. Over the next twenty minutes, they peeled away one item of clothing at a time until they were down to bikinis. The guys went wild. I have no idea why. Lieutenant Anderson must need glasses. To me, these women were old and ugly. Their bodies had seen much better days. But the guys didn't seem to care probably because most were already drunk. I was close behind.

By midnight, everyone was happy. Mike was happiest of all. He was so happy, he didn't notice that his future brothers-in-law had locked a real ball and chain to his right ankle. As he went from table to table to thank guys, he dragged it behind him. Everyone laughed, even Mike.

As I sank into the back seat of a taxi, I was happy too. I was beyond happy. I was drunk and so drunk that I don't remember how the taxi found its way to my home or what it cost.

It seemed that a matter of minutes passed before my mother's voice woke me.

"Aren't you supposed to be in a wedding today?"

My eyes seemed to be stuck shut. My head felt like it was twice its size. My forehead throbbed like it had never throbbed before. My throat was parched. When I tried to speak, what came out sounded like I had laryngitis.

"By the sound of you, I can only guess that the party was a success."

Although she was a soft-spoken woman, that morning my mother's voice sounded like she had launched a fifty-megaton bomb next to my ears.

"I'll get you a cup of black coffee and some aspirins. A shower will help too." While I was grateful for her attention, I wished she knew how to whisper.

As I threw back the covers on my bed, it was difficult for me to move my limbs. They were stiff and sore. Besides too much beer, I wondered what else I had done the previous night. Nothing came to mind as I lumbered into the bathroom. It took all my energy to turn the shower knob. Rather than wait to test the water temperature, I stepped in. The cold water against my body was a shock, and by the time the water warmed, I was awake. I felt terrible. I couldn't feel worse. So I knew that today could only get better. It had to. It was Mike's big day, and I was his best man.

After a few cups of black coffee, I started to feel human again. My mother had pressed my tuxedo shirt. As she handed it to me, she said, "I want you to be the most handsome man at the wedding." Although my brain activity was still weak, I had no doubts about my appearance. Once I buttoned the jacket on my pale blue tuxedo and looked in the full-length mirror on the back of my bedroom door, I knew I looked great. I felt better too.

My dad drove me to Alf's so I could pick up my car. From Alf's, it wasn't far to the church. I could see the other groomsmen as I parked my car. They looked good too. We shook hands. Compared to the previous night, we were subdued.

"How's Mike?"

The guys broke their silence and started to chuckle.

"What so funny?" I asked.

Johnny explained that it took Mike most of the morning to get the ball and chain off his ankle. "We don't know how he slept with that thing on. His mom and dad weren't impressed. And when Tonya heard about it, she went berserk."

We all roared with laughter. Tonya's other brother, Tony, said, "That was a helluva party, Willis. You raised a ton of money for Mike. I hope you'll plan my bachelor party if I ever decide to get married."

The ceremony went off without a hitch. It was fast compared to the amount of time it took for the photographs after. The ceremony took less than half an hour, while the photography session took almost two hours. How can one photographer come up with so many poses? I started to feel like a contortionist and had no idea why he made us travel from the church to a park. Call me crazy, but I thought his focus should have been directed toward the bride and groom not the trees, flowers, and fountains in the park.

After we finished with the photographs, we headed to the reception hall. I was parched and hungry. Thankfully, the reception took care of both needs, although I couldn't face a beer when it was offered. Even the smell of champagne made my stomach do flip flops. I suffered through the toasts. Mine to the bride and groom was short and sweet but heartfelt.

After the meal and toasts, the music started. It was loud, and my head wasn't ready for it. It still ached. By the winces on the groomsmen's faces, their heads weren't ready either. As the night wore on, the music bothered me less. I even danced with the bride and Mike's mother. It would have been nice to dance with the bridesmaids and other female guests, but I ran out of steam. The bachelor party had done me in. It was a disappointment especially when I looked so good. What a waste of a great tuxedo. I wouldn't repeat that mistake. If ever a friend asked to be a best man again, I would hold his bachelor party at least a week before the big day.

7

Mrs. McIntyre

After I claimed my coffee at McDonald's drive-through window, I stopped by my office to pick up file number 16-12-07MCI and headed out to meet Mrs. McIntyre. Traffic was heavier on Interstate 80 than I expected so it took me almost 25 minutes to reach her home. It didn't matter because I always allow extra time. Besides, while I finished my coffee, I wanted to give myself enough time to review the file. I also wanted to formulate some sort of discussion game plan for that morning's appointment with Mrs. McIntyre. I didn't have much to go on, so my plan took more time to develop than usual.

I still had twenty minutes before our appointment was scheduled to begin. During my wait, as I thought about the discussion to take place, I stared at her home and the ones around her. The neighborhood was how I remembered it. As a police officer, it was an area we drove through but had no reason to stop. The homes on those ten city streets are the most expensive in the city. They're called the "Fabulous Forties" for a reason. Former Governor Ronald Reagan lived here for most of his term. People who own homes here know whom or what doesn't fit in. They don't hesitate to call the police if they see someone or something suspicious. As a result, criminals and outsiders know to stay away.

Mrs. McIntyre's home is strategically placed at the top of the arc of a circular driveway. Hers is Spanish style and two stories high. The stucco is painted in what I would call pale pink, although I'm sure Sherwin-Williams or Benjamin Moore have more impressive names for colors that add beauty to houses in neighborhoods like this one. The lower half of each window, both upper and lower stories, have what looks like short black metal fences. Each slat in the wrought iron fence is turned slightly and shaped like an elongated letter *s.* On other homes, these fences may be installed for security purposes, but on this one, I suspected they had been installed for decorative purposes only because a similar version covers the small window in her front door. No one could have fit through that window regardless of any security measures. Below the window is a wrought iron door knocker in a similar turned style.

I noticed the lawns around the driveway and on either side of the house were manicured to perfection. No blade of grass was out of place. They looked like a gardener had trimmed them with scissors. The hedges, shrubs, bushes, and flowers complemented the house too. They had been planted with equal care.

As I sat behind the wheel of my black Ford Crown Victoria, I continued to examine the exterior of Mrs. McIntyre's home and yard. Old habits die hard. As a cop, I was trained and conditioned to take note of even the smallest detail.

From the driveway to the front door, I saw a walkway and wide set of stairs constructed out of slate. On each side of the front door were two dark-blue ceramic planters. I guessed they were at least five feet high. In the morning sun, they glistened like the spray from ocean waves.

From my vantage point, I couldn't see a garage. Then I remembered most of the houses on these streets access their garages from laneways behind their homes. In any other part of the city, these laneways are called alleyways. In addition to their cars, which they kept out of view, residents house their trash cans. These are emptied twice per week by an anonymous company. No one sees or cares how it's done along as it's done. Unlike small children at dinner tables who should be seen but not heard, garbage trucks are heard but they never seen on these city streets.

I glanced at my wristwatch. It was now ten o'clock and time to meet with Mrs. McIntyre. I crumpled my napkin, deposited it in my empty paper coffee cup, and put the lid back on. I would dispose of it later. Then I picked up the file folder from the front passenger seat, got out of my car, closed the door, pressed the lock button on my key fob, and headed for Mrs. McIntyre's front door. The wrought iron door knocker was every bit as impressive and heavy as it looked from the street. I rapped it twice. The front door opened and I was greeted by a woman who, based on her appearance, was Mrs. McIntyre not household help.

"Mr. Prescott?"

"Yes, Mrs. McIntyre?"

"Yes, I am pleased to make your acquaintance. I am pleased you agreed to discuss my son's case. I have set up coffee for us in the sunroom where I believe we'll be more comfortable."

Mrs. McIntyre turned to lead the way. I closed the door behind me as I watched her start to walk down a long hallway.

As I followed Mrs. McIntyre, I peaked in the rooms on either side of the hall. To my left, I saw a large living room with two sofas that faced each other. I captured a glimpse of a fireplace, along with a separate area that had two arm chairs and a round table between them. The draperies and upholstery were like something I've only seen in expensive hotels—opulent. To my right, I noticed an equally large dining room. Over the long table hung a huge crystal chandelier. Before I moved on, I counted at least ten chairs placed at the table. The walls were paneled two-thirds up in dark wood. On the way to the sunroom, we passed through the kitchen. It looked like something I might see in Architectural Digest. Unlike my home, the stainless steel appliances were top of the line and they matched.

The sunroom was at the far end of the kitchen. Because it looked different from the rest of the house, it may have been an add-on. The room had windows on all three sides plus a glass ceiling. Under the windows were bench seats. The room held a round table, plus two additional arm chairs. The floral fabric on the chairs matched the fabric on the bench seats and the draperies that hung on each side of the windows. It was a bright and cheerful room but too feminine for my taste. Mrs. McIntyre offered me a chair. However, before I took my place, I held the back of other chair for her. Once we were both seated, she offered me coffee from the service that had set up on a tray in the middle of the table. Then, she offered me cookies from a small tray.

As we sipped our coffees and after I tasted the best chocolate chip cookie in my lifetime, I complimented Mrs. McIntyre on her home. I told how much the beauty of her garden impressed me. For the first time, I saw her smile, a pleasant one revealing dimples in her cheeks and pearl white straight teeth. It's difficult for me to describe Mrs. McIntyre. Whenever I spent time with her, she was well dressed, well coiffed, and made up. I could tell Mrs. McIntyre looked after herself.

To an old movie buff like me, she reminds me of Olivia de Havilland, but her voice reminds me of Lauren Bacall. I can't think of any current actress to whom I could compare her, which doesn't say much for the depth of today's movie stars. The best I can come up with is a combination of many actresses: Mrs. McIntyre seemed to have the reserve of Nicole Kidman, the facial countenance and coloring of Annette Bening, the overall stature of Helen Mirren, and the voice of a Kathleen Turner when Kathleen Turner was younger. Yet all of these comparisons are a disservice to Mrs. McIntyre. She is more elegant than any woman on today's big screen.

Mrs. McIntyre explained that she employed a gardener who had been with the family for many years.

"My husband and I inherited this house from his parents, who in turn had inherited from his grandparents. His grandparents had the house built in the early 1930s. I had hoped to pass the house onto my son."

As she mentioned her son, I saw Mrs. McIntyre's eyes start to tear and her lips start to quiver, but she managed to keep her composure. "Perhaps we could review all the documents and items I have about my son's murder. I know your time is important to you, and I don't want to waste yours or mine."

From then on, Mrs. McIntyre was all business. As she picked up a thick folder, I picked up my pen and pulled out my pad of lined paper. She opened the folder and explained that it contained police and medical examiner reports. The file was about two inches thick, which suggested to me that both the police department and medical examiner's office had been thorough.

"Mr. Prescott, I am lending this file to you in order that you may review it and copy any items that you believe are pertinent to your examination of my son's case, but I want it back within three days. My attorney has prepared an agreement with respect to this file and the other items I plan to share with you this morning. If you take the file and the items, we ask that you sign this receipt, which specifies the items you have taken and when you will return them."

An agreement presented by a client for me to sign was a new experience. Most often, I presented a services and fee agreement for the client to sign. I nodded my head.

Next, Mrs. McIntyre picked up a paper bag. She opened it and removed a shirt, slacks, and shoes. "Our funeral director gave me this bag of clothing when I came to view Jamie's body. The medical examiner had included these clothes and shoes with Jamie's watch and wallet when the funeral home picked up Jamie's body. These, Mr. Prescott, more than anything else in that file, prove to me that my son was murdered." The confused look on my face must have given me away. "Mr. Prescott, I can assure you that my son would never wear that shirt, those pants, or those shoes. I knew the watch was his because my husband and I gave it to Jamie on his twenty- first birthday. And I know the wallet was his because I have seen it before and it has all his iden- tification and credit cards inside. But, these clothes—these awful, awful clothes—were things my son would never ever wear. He took great pride in his appearance."

Mrs. McIntyre became more and more agitated and emphatic. But as she spoke, she impressed me more and more. When she brought up the clothes, anyone else might have looked askance. However, as a clothes horse, I could understand her point of view. Although I knew enough not to say it, I thought it. I wouldn't have been caught dead in those clothes either.

"Mr. Prescott, the police believe that my son's death was caused by a drunk driver. They have ruled it was an accident. Worse, the police have now closed its file despite my repeated appeals to investigate my son's death further. They won't listen to me, and now they won't respond to my calls. During my last discussion with Lieutenant White, he suggested that if I wanted to continue to pursue this case, I should hire a private investigator. When I asked him whom he would recommend, Lieutenant White gave me your name and number. He is why I called you. Will you take my case?"

As much as I appreciated Mike's referral, I wondered why he would expect me to waste my time if the case was closed? Why would he think that I would want to spin my wheels? Why not give out the name of another private investigator if all he wanted to do was get Mrs. McIntyre off his back? Maybe that was it. Maybe Mike thought I would take a look at the case, support him and the police, advise Mrs. McIntyre so that she would back off, and, at the same time, collect a fee. I didn't know what to think, but I would call Mike just as soon as I examined everything Mrs. McIntyre gave me. Over the next few days, I hoped that this case, if there was a case, would become clearer.

In response to her question, I decided it was best to hedge my bets. After all, her agreement gave me three days to mull this case over.

"Mrs. McIntyre, I will be happy to sign the agreement your attorney has prepared for you. Today, my plan is to take the items you have shared and examine them over the three days you have allotted to me. At the end of those three days, I will give you an opinion as to how I believe we should continue. If what I recommend to you sounds reasonable, I have a copy of my investigative services agreement for you to sign. I propose that you pay me a retainer of five hundred dollars. As I review everything, my time will be charged against this retainer. My rate is seventy-five dollars per hour, plus any expenses. If, at the end of three days, you decide not continue, I will refund any balance that is owed to you.

If we decide to go ahead, my fees over and above the retainer will be billed to you on a monthly basis. Is this acceptable?"

Without hesitation, Mrs. McIntyre accepted my proposal. As I signed her agreement and handed it to her, she signed my agreement and a check for my retainer. She handed both to me. While we drank our second cup of coffee, I asked Mrs. McIntyre to tell me all about her son. Her expression softened. Even though her eyes welled, her lips didn't quiver this time. Instead her face brightened.

"Mr. Prescott, my son was the most wonderful son a mother could ever have. He was as considerate as he was handsome and successful. Jamie called me every day without fail."

I asked Mrs. McIntyre what her son did and where he lived.

"Right after Jamie graduated from Stanford, with his degree in business and computer science, he went to work for a software company in San Jose. He worked with a team of people, like him, who created games for computers and mobile phones. His work was something I really didn't understand, but he must have been good at it. Within two years, he left the company, moved back here, and started his own business. Not more than three months went by before Jamie sold his first program. He called it an "app." Jamie never looked back. When he was killed, Jamie was doing well. He had just bought a new car. And I believe that he had fifteen employees who worked for him."

By the enthusiasm in her voice and the animation in her face, I could tell Mrs. McIntyre loved her son. She didn't hold back.

"When Jamie moved back to the city, he lived with me for a couple of months. It was nice to see him back in his old bedroom. I enjoyed his company and the chance to cook and clean for him again. But I knew he wanted his own place.

While I wanted him to buy a house nearby, Jamie wanted to buy a condominium on the top floor of the highest building in Downtown Sacramento. Jamie wanted to be near all the restaurants and the action. Jamie told me he was a "foodie," which always made me smile because I could never get him to try anything new or finish a meal when he was a child. Jamie seemed to date quite a bit, although I didn't meet many of his girlfriends unless he seemed serious. Then he would mention them in our daily calls, and he might bring them home to meet me. I do think he was serious about his last one, Lilly Chin. He brought her to the house several times for dinner or just to visit. Lilly was a very pretty girl. I hoped that, one day, Jamie would marry and have children of his own. I really hoped to be a grandmother one day."

As she finished, Mrs. McIntyre's lips now trembled. She held back her tears. I expressed my sorrow for her loss and assured her I would do all I could for her, although I wasn't sure yet that was.

It was now nearly noon. I asked Mrs. McIntyre where and when she wanted to meet three days from now. We agreed to meet at her home again but, next time, at two p.m. I pulled her documents and bag of clothes together. "Mrs. McIntyre, do you have access to Jamie's condominium?"

"Yes, as a matter of fact I do. I'm not sure what to do about it yet. Why do you ask, Mr. Prescott?"

"I'd like to go in and take a look around. It may help me get a better sense of what may have happened to Jamie."

As I stood, Mrs. McIntyre handed me the key to her son's condominium. We shook hands, and I saw myself out the front door. As I slipped underneath the steering wheel of my car, I put my file and everything else on the passenger seat and wondered where all of this was going to lead, if anywhere.

8

Mike White

On my way back to the office, I returned to McDonald's and exchanged that morning's trash along with some cash for a Big Mac, French fries, and large Coke. While I sat at my desk and ate my meal, I reflected on my time with Mrs. McIntyre. She impressed me. Despite her grief, I found she was composed and forthright about her son's death. It was clear to me that Mrs. McIntyre believed her son was murdered despite what the police department told her. It was also clear to me, no matter what the police department ruled, her son's file would remain open in her mind until she found out who murdered him.

As I dipped a French fry into ketchup, I couldn't decide whether to read her documents first and call Mike after or call Mike first and read her documents after. If I read everything first, I would know more about the case and would be in a better position to ask Mike more and better questions about the file. On the other hand, if I met with Mike first, I could get an overall sense of the case from him and read the documents with the benefit of his knowledge and perspective. Of course, that meant I would also have his biases when I reviewed Mrs. McIntyre's file. As I chewed my French fry, I decided to meet with Mike first. If, after I read

Mrs. McIntyre's documents I needed greater clarity, I could always meet with Mike again.

I picked up my telephone and called Mike. He answered on the first ring.

"Hey, Will, what's up?"

"Hey yourself, what's your schedule like? Can we get together this week for a drink?"

"Sure, Will, how about later today. Why don't we meet at Alf's around five?"

"Sounds good, Mike. I'll see you at five."

Our telephone call lasted less than thirty seconds. I couldn't tell by the sound of Mike's voice if he was curious why I called, if he was happy to get to together for a drink, or both. Regardless, I always enjoyed our times together and any chance to catch up. But, more importantly, I also wanted to find out why he referred me to Mrs. McIntyre and discover what he had to say about Jamie McIntyre's death. His comments would help me determine how to proceed.

For the rest the afternoon, I decided to head home and take a nap before I met Mike. I considered afternoon naps and golf games two of the great joys of business ownership. While the police force offered many benefits, my time was determined by SPD not by me. Now that I was in business for myself, my time on the job was determined by me not by SPD. I reveled in the freedom my business gave me, especially when, thanks to Mrs. McIntyre, I had a check for five hundred dollars in my back pocket.

The alarm buzzed at four o'clock. Within twenty minutes, I showered, dressed, and headed off to meet Mike. Because of afternoon rush-hour traffic, I needed all of the forty minutes that remained to arrive on time. As I pulled into Alf's parking lot, I could see Mike's car in my rear- view mirror. I raised my right hand and waved. I could see him smile.

"How's that for punctuality?" asked Mike as he closed and locked his car door.

Mike looked a whole lot different now than he did when he graduated from the police academy. Unlike me, but like a lot of men his age, he had a paunch, which made it difficult for him to keep his trousers around his waist. I was grateful that he gave up his combover and let what we referred to as his "chrome dome" shine through. Although Mike had lost most of the hair on his head, he made up for the shortfall with a big mustache on his upper lip. I've seen walruses with less hair. Despite the changes in his girth and hairline, Mike still had a great smile that, to me, always revealed an open heart.

Most often Mike and I sat at the bar. That day, though, I steered him toward a table for two. I wanted to have a one-on-one and confidential discussion. In a place like Alf's, I knew that both would be difficult to achieve, but they would be even more difficult if we were seated at the bar. Mike didn't seem to take any notice. We both ordered draft beers from our server. I asked Mike if he wanted something to eat.

"Nah, Tonya expects me home for dinner, which is funny because she knows I'm out with you. By now, you'd think she'd know better than to expect me home at a decent time."

We both chuckled. Despite our guffaws, I respected and admired Mike's marriage to Tonya. They made it work. My marriages, all three of them, had been busts. As a result, I didn't want to make Mike late and make Tonya angry with him or with me, so I got down to business. "I met with Mrs. McIntyre today." Mike didn't react. "She told me that you referred her to me. She also told me that the police depart-ment closed the file on her son's case. So, Mike, why did you give Mrs. McIntyre my name on a case you closed? She's a nice lady. I hope it wasn't your idea of a joke."

My voice wasn't antagonistic. Instead, I spoke in a matter-of-fact tone. It didn't matter. I saw Mike flinch. It was obvious that my comments hit a nerve. Mike leaned back in his chair as he tried to recover. I could tell by his reactions that he knew that ours was no longer a causal get-together.

Mike cleared his throat, took a swig of his beer, and swallowed hard. "Sorry, Will. When I told Mrs. McIntyre that as far as we were concerned, her son's case was closed, I knew she wasn't happy, but I thought she would eventually come to terms with our conclusion about his death. So when she asked me if I knew a private detective, yours was the only name that came to mind. I didn't think for a second she would actually call you. If so, I would have let you know. Trust me, it was no joke. I spent weeks with that woman. When it came to her son's death, she was like a dog with a bone. No matter how we tried to explain it, Mrs. McIntyre wouldn't accept that her son's death was the result of an accident. We showed her all the evidence to no avail. I wish now that I had given you a heads-up, but I really didn't think she'd call you."

Mike was earnest in his response. I believed him and told him so. We sat and sipped our beers and stared at the table for a few minutes.

Mike spoke first. "Will, I gotta tell ya, Jamie McIntyre's case was a slam dunk. The woman who hit him blew twice the legal limit. I could smell the alcohol on her breath an hour after the accident. She was as drunk as a skunk. I'm not sure of her name now. It sounded French. I think it was Monique or something like that. Of course, it wasn't enough that she hit him and drove for another twenty-five feet, she backed up and ran over him again. Jamie McIntyre's body was pretty roughed up: first by the impact of the car and then by its undercarriage. When I arrived on the scene, Dr. Overstreet from the medical examiner's office had already pronounced him dead. The police, who arrived before I did, had taken statements from everyone. There were no witnesses, although drivers from the vehicles that came upon the accident rushed to offer aid and call 911. That Monique woman was a strange one, a real fruitcake. She insisted that she had been distracted by a big white animal that looked like a ghost. Most drunks claim to see pink elephants, but not her. She said she saw an animal or a ghost that she couldn't describe other than to say it was white."

I asked Mike if any of the other drivers had seen a big white animal or anything else suspicious that night. Mike sighed. "Jesus, Will, give me a break. The woman was drunk. Nothing she said made sense. We weren't about to start a search based on anything she had to say."

I also asked Mike about the clothes Jamie McIntyre wore that night. "Will, who knows why Jamie McIntyre was dressed the way he was dressed. We aren't the fashion police, for Christ's sake. We're the real police, you know, the kind who trained at the academy, gained experience, and have badges to prove it."

I decided not to ask Mike any more questions. He had become agitated and defensive. Who could blame him? Mike is a rock solid cop who always follows procedure. In his shoes, I wouldn't like to be questioned either.

"Will, do you remember what Chief Detective Don Black drilled into us? He always said that every case is like an orange. It has ten segments and each one of those segments has to be assessed in order to conduct a thorough investigation."

"Yeah, Mike. I remember. Who could forget? At least once a week, the chief would tell us each case was just like an orange. Then, he would hold up his fists and enumerate each section, finger by finger. I used to wonder why he didn't bring in a real orange for effect. Instead, he always started with the thumb of his right hand. He called it 'how.' It was how followed by 'who,' 'what,' 'when,' and 'where' until all five fingers of his left hand were exposed. Then, he lifted the thumb of his left hand. He called it 'motive.' It was followed by 'evidence,' 'interpretation,' 'coordination,' and 'deduction.' When he had accounted for all ten segments and had fingers up, he'd clap his hands and tell us to get to work. For over seven years, I heard him make that corny reference to an orange and its segments. After seven years, every file I picked up started to smell like Minute Maid. Where did he find that crazy analogy anyway? Did anyone check if an orange has ten segments?"

"Yep, I did, Will. I searched the Internet and most oranges do have ten segments. The chief was on to something. You may not have liked his orange analogy, but I have relied on it and those ten basic segments ever since. They have stood me in good stead. I always think of them whenever I am assigned to a new case. They remind me to be thorough whenever I conduct an investigation. I can't believe that you don't think of those orange segments when you investigate."

"I used to but not anymore. When I started my own business, I also started to leave the constraints of police department policies and procedures behind. Over time, I learned that every case is different and has to be approached in different ways. Don't get me wrong; Chief Black's approach has value and I always take his segments into account. But his approach can limit an investigation. I believe each case is more like an onion than an orange. An onion has many layers that need to be peeled away in order to get to the core rather than ten predefined segments. That's the approach I use now when I am hired to investigate any case. And, let's face it, I have to have a different approach than the police department. When clients like Mrs. McIntyre hire me, it's often because they have been disillusioned or disappointed by their police departments."

"So, Will, even after I explained our investigation into Jamie McIntyre's case, does this mean you plan to look at it like, as you say, an onion?" I nodded my head. "I can't believe it, Will. You and I have worked together for years. Don't you trust what I have just told you? Can't you accept that Jamie McIntyre's death was an accident?"

"Mike, I do trust you. I don't know yet if I will pursue this case. I've got some legwork to do over the next few days. But, yeah, if I decide to take the case, I will treat it like an onion and peel away each layer until I get to its base. The base may look like the results of your investigation or it might look like something different. I'm sorry if that offends you. But remember, you referred Mrs. McIntyre to me. I didn't look for her or this case."

Mike sighed and shook his head. By his expression, I knew he wasn't pleased. In order to change the subject, I asked him how many fish he caught over the last few weeks. In the past, Mike's eyes would light up when I asked him about his favorite sport. Not that day. As we finished our beers, Mike muttered something, but his answer was per-functory. He gave off a vibe that led me to believe that Mrs. McIntyre's case might change our relationship. My next thought sounded corny even to me. I wondered, if I peeled this onion, would tears follow?

9

File No. 16-12-07MCI

Even though my discussion with Mike left me uncomfortable, I had to set any concerns aside. I had a job to do. It was time to review all Mrs. McIntyre's information about her son's death. I had to look at it with dispassion. And, yes, my initial review would rely on the ten investigatory segments that Chief Don Black had drilled into me and all the other detectives on the squad. As they say, old habits die hard. But my gut instincts told me that this case had more layers to it than Mike or anyone else in his department could see.

For the first time, I opened Mrs. McIntyre's folder. I had to hand it to her. Her file folder was better organized than any others I have ever seen before. Sometimes, all I get is an envelope or a shoe box full of papers. Every piece of paper in Mrs. McIntyre's folder had been two-hole punched and secured with a metal clasp at the top of the file. Mrs. McIntyre was meticulous. I was impressed.

The first document I saw was a certificate of death. It was a standard government form, U.S. Standard Certificate of Death Rev. 11/2003. I was surprised it showed that the standard document had been revised in November 2003. It looked just like the one from before 2003, except it was now letter size rather than legal size. Most cities and states throughout the country use this form rather than create their own. Why reinvent the wheel? To help reduce confusion about decedents with the same names, the form allows for a local file number on the left-hand side at the top, and the form allows for a state file number on the right-hand side at the top. I looked at those numbers, and based on my experience, they looked appropriate—nothing amiss. To this day, I am not sure how cities, counties, and states come up with their file systems. I wish they were as simple to understand as mine.

I reviewed the fifty plus items on the form. As usual, the funeral director completed the first twenty-three items. These items, as you might expect, include the decedent's legal name (in this case, "James John McIntyre"), sex ("male"), age last birthday ("27"), and other statistical information like date of birth, residence, marital status, father's name, mother's name, location of death, and location of burial. As usual, the funeral director also completed items fifty-one through fifty-five. These relate to the decedent's education, race, and occupation. I'm not sure why our government puts these items at the end of the form. To me, it would make more sense to put them together with all the decedent's other information at the top of the form. Despite my issue with the form design, my review found no issues with the funeral director's statements. They were routine.

I turned my attention to items twenty-four through fifty. This is the area that must be completed by what our government calls a medical certifier. In part of the country, we call the medical certifier, the chief medical examiner. In Sacramento, his name is Dr. Henry Ortega. The medical examiner may complete the form or assign any one of his licensed assistant medical examiners. On this part of the form is where I had hoped to find more about Jamie McIntyre's death. I hoped to see the results of Dr. Ortega's examination.

Over the years as a police detective, I had many occasions to meet with Dr. Ortega. We had formed a good professional relationship. I respected him and I believe he respected me. As such, I was confident he would speak to me if I needed more information.

When I looked at the certificate of death, I was surprised to see a name that I didn't recognize. Instead of Dr. Ortega, items twenty-six, forty-five, forty-six, and forty-seven showed Dr. Miles Overstreet as the medical certifier. I wondered when he joined the medical examiner's office. Before I stopped by to introduce myself to Dr. Overstreet, I would conduct some research on him based on his license number shown under item twenty-seven.

For now, I turned my attention to item thirty-two, part 1, which is referred to as "Known Cause of Death." As the "Immediate Cause of Death," Dr. Overstreet listed a fractured skull, crushed chest, severe external trauma, and collision with a motor vehicle. As the "Approximate Interval: Onset to Death," Dr. Overstreet listed minutes. Next, I turned my attention to item forty-seven, which is referred to as "Manner of Death." Dr. Overstreet filled in the box next to "Accident."

Lorna McIntyre informed me that Jamie was in good health when he died. So it was no surprise to see that Dr. Overstreet listed no other underlying causes or condition that may have contributed to Jamie McIntyre's death, such as heart disease, diabetes or tobacco use.

All in all, the certificate of death was straightforward. Both the funeral director and medical examiner had completed their sections of the form in accordance with policies and procedures.

I photocopied the certificate of death and set it aside to place in my file folder later. The next item in Mrs. McIntyre's folder was the police department's report. It confirmed all that Mike had shared with me over drinks. With respect to Jamie McIntyre, the officer who was first to arrive on the scene called in several codes. The first code was 11-42, which means an ambulance is not required. The second code was 11-44, which means fatality. Another code was 11-98, which means meet officer, followed by code 11-85, which means tow truck needed, and 10-15X, which meant a female prisoner. The first officer on the scene was thorough, and his thoroughness was reflected in the report. As the officer in charge, Mike's part of the report was just as thorough. I could find no fault with their report. They had completed it in accordance with all policies and procedures.

I photocopied the police report and set it aside to place in my file folder at a later time. The next items were photographs of the accident scene. I don't how or why Mrs. McIntyre obtained these. The photographs were gruesome reminders of a horrible event. They upset me to look at them. I couldn't begin to imagine how they must affect her.

As I studied each photograph, I grabbed the paper bag and removed the clothes and shoes Jamie McIntyre wore the night of the accident. I wanted to compare the clothes in the photographs to the clothes in the bag. I also wanted to gain a broader perspective of the accident scene. The clothes in the photograph matched the clothes in the bag. The size of the clothes confirmed that Jamie McIntyre was a slender man of average height. The reports showed his height as five feet, eight inches tall and his weight at one hundred and forty-eight pounds. Although the bag contained a pair of men's shoes, the photographs did not show any. Was this because the photographer recorded the scene from angles in which the shoes were not apparent? Or was it because Jamie McIntyre's had lost his shoes upon impact with the vehicle? I would have to check.

The sizes of the clothes coincided with someone of Jamie McIntyre's build. The shirt label was marked "M" and the trouser label showed thirty-two waist and twenty-nine length. The labels on the shirt and pants revealed brands from discount stores. Based on what his mother told me, the brands and types of clothes in the bag were not the kinds anyone would associate with a man of Jamie McIntyre's taste and budget. Unlike the shirt and pants, the size of the shoes did not coincide with someone of Jamie McIntyre's build. They were marked "11.5 W." To me, these were too long and wide. Further, the shoes were a brand I didn't recognize and they were constructed of man-made materials. I would have to find out Jamie McIntyre's shoe size. The shoes raised a red flag for me. I wondered if the medical examiner's office had made a mistake and placed the wrong shoes in the bag assigned to Jamie McIntyre. If so, I wondered if the medical examiner's office made other errors when they handled Jamie McIntyre's body.

I photocopied the photographs and set them aside to place in my file folder later. Before I closed Mrs. McIntyre's folder, I flipped through the rest of the pages to get a sense of what was left to review. Invoices from the funeral home, cemetery, and tow truck company popped out at me. I decided they could wait for review. It was now time for me to gain more first-hand knowledge about Jamie McIntyre. I picked up my car keys and the key to his condominium. I needed to see where and how Jamie McIntyre lived.

10

Jamie McIntyre

It was just after noon as I exited my office lot. My stomach rumbled. I had plenty of time to reach Jamie McIntyre's condominium before rush hour started. So I decided to stop for a bite to eat. As much as McDonald's tempted me, I decided to visit another place. I pulled into the strip mall just before the freeway entrance and parked in front of my favorite diner—Perky's, although not much about it could be called perky. The pattern on the Formica tabletops has been washed off over the years, and if you're lucky, you might find a red vinyl chair without a tear in its seat or back. The servers are all women. They wear uniforms from a bygone era and walk like they're past their prime. That's because they are past their prime. Most have worked for Perky's since it opened over thirty years ago. Nonetheless, the food is terrific, which is why so many of us have become what the servers call "regulars." We return time and time again for the food if not the service.

To place my order, I didn't need to look at the menu. I knew every page of the menu off by heart. It hadn't changed in over thirty years either. I ordered a small tossed salad without the pickled beets. Perky's doesn't offer a choice of salad dressings. It has one kind, which at Perky's is "French" dressing. Regular customers, like me, call it "pink stuff."

That day, I wanted to order stuffed bell peppers, as they are my favorites. However, I knew they could cause indigestion, which I didn't need that afternoon or any afternoon for that matter. Instead, I ordered a hot turkey sandwich with mashed potatoes and gravy. I told my server, Gladys, to hold the green beans.

"No problem," she said and then asked, "Do you want dessert?"

Why not? I ordered a piece of lemon meringue pie.

I was hungrier than I had thought. I polished off the salad and the turkey dinner in no time at all. They hit the spot. As I sipped my third cup of coffee, I was aware the better part of two days had gone by. In that time, not one thing led me to believe that Jamie McIntyre's death had been anything but an accident. I wondered what I was going to tell Mrs. McIntyre on day three. My thoughts were interrupted by Gladys, who brought me a nice big wedge of pie. It was super sweet and tart at the same time. For me, it was a perfect end to a perfect meal. My stomach was settled, but my mind was uncertain about this case. After a big meal, I might have been tempted to take a nap. But, though, I knew I needed to learn more about Jamie McIntyre.

As I pulled onto the freeway, traffic was still light and I was able to move over to the fast lane with ease. I made it into the city in less than twenty minutes. It took me as long to find a place to park near Jamie McIntyre's condominium. After several trips around the block, I saw a car pull out of a spot, and I pulled right in behind it. My lucky day! The meter showed time available, although not enough time for me to complete my examination of the condominium. I deposited a couple of quarters into the slot and I wound up with about two hours of time, which I thought should be enough. I grabbed my blazer from the hook over the back seat window, put it on, straightened my tie, locked my car, and headed across the street to the condominium.

As I entered the lobby, I noticed a man in a uniform seated behind a desk. I approached him with my hand outstretched. He stood and extended his.

"Hello, my name is Willis Prescott. I have been retained by Mrs. Lorna McIntyre. She has given me a key to her late son's condo. I'm here to take a look inside."

While he shook my hand, the man in uniform introduced himself as Joe Lawrence. "I'm the doorman, Mr. Prescott. Mrs. McIntyre called to let me know ya might stop by. She's a nice woman that Mrs. McIntyre. I sure feel sorry for her. Her son was nice too. He always smiled, said hello, and asked me about my family. He was one of the few around here that did. I miss him. You go on up to his place and, if I can help ya, just let me know when ya come back down. I'm on duty until six o'clock. The elevators are in the hall behind me. Mr. McIntyre's condo is on the top floor. As you step off the elevator, turn right. His is at the end of the hallway."

I nodded and thanked Joe as I walked away. I found three sets of elevator doors on the far wall in the hallway. I pressed the button, and within seconds, the middle door opened. It was empty. I boarded and pressed fourteen. The elevator made no other stops on the way up to the fourteenth floor. As the doors opened, I noticed that the walls in front of me were wallpapered and the hallway floor was carpeted. Both were luxurious. They reminded me of what I might see in Mrs. McIntyre's house. I turned right as Joe Lawrence had instructed me and headed to the last unit on the floor. I inserted the key in the lock. It turned so I knew I had the right condominium. As I entered, I was surprised by the contrast of this unit to the building's hallway. As plush as the hallway was decorated, the condo was stark by comparison.

Right away, I could tell Jamie McIntyre's taste was minimal yet tasteful. His floors were finished in a light-colored hardwood, probably maple based on the small amount of grain in each board. The walls were painted white, but I detected a slight hue that I was certain that he or his decorator selected to complement the floor. His living room furniture was modern. The sofa was upholstered in white leather and stood on chrome legs. Opposite the sofa was a leather chair and ottoman, Both matched the sofa. Next to the chair was a light-colored rattan chair which, as I turned my eyes toward the dining area, I could tell complemented the chairs around the glass top and chrome table. I have no idea who painted the pictures on the wall. They were huge, colorful, and abstract.

Although the condominium unit screamed modern, it possessed a quiet elegance. Behind the sofa was a wall outfitted with what I would call an entertainment center constructed of glass and chrome. This center included a glass-top desk, which was situated between two sets of bookshelves. The bookshelves to the left of the desktop held some books, but more prominent was a Bose music system and speakers. The bookshelves to the right of the desktop held a few more books, as well as some small sculptures, art pieces, and a computer printer. I turned my attention to the desktop, which, except for two power chords, one small square box of Kleenex, two mechanical pencils and a ballpoint pen, was empty. A laptop was nowhere to be seen. I made a mental note to ask Mrs. McIntyre about her son's computers.

Beyond the glass-top tables and five chairs in the dining area, I saw a mirrored credenza against the wall that separated this area from the kitchen. It looked as modern as the other pieces in the living room. As I moved closer to it, I saw that the credenza had a small drawer in its center. I opened it. Inside were two boxes of table coasters, a bottle opener, a corkscrew, silver ice cube tongs, and four packages of cocktail napkins, all of which looked like they were embossed with witticisms. On top of the credenza was a large rectangle tray. It was constructed of mirrored glass too. On top of the tray were various bottles of liquor—all expensive brands of single malt scotch, vodka, gin, whiskey and aperitifs. These led me to believe that Jamie McIntyre liked to imbibe alcoholic beverages. I reminded myself to check for toxicology data in the medical examiner's report.

Jamie McIntyre's condominium was the type of place you might find featured in Architectural Digest. In no way did it resemble his mother's home, yet it showed the same kind of sophistication. Beyond the dining area was the kitchen. The cabinets and countertops were white too, although all the appliances were high-end stainless steel. I discovered a stainless steel wine refrigerator with a clear glass front below the counter. It was filled with white wines. I'm not a wine drinker, but based on his choices in liquor, I assumed that the wines were expensive brands too. When I opened the door to the pantry, I discovered another stainless steel wine refrigerator. This one held red wines only. The pantry was also stocked with canned goods, as well as various snacks: cans of peanuts and bags of potato and nacho chips. The large kitchen refrigerator held cans of beer with names I didn't recognize, along with assorted sodas and mixers. I suspected Jamie McIntyre drank gin and tonic based on the number of tonic bottles in his refrigerator. Overall, the kitchen was as immaculate as the living and dining rooms.

To the right of the kitchen entrance was a hallway, which led to a bathroom on the left and a guest bedroom on the right. The master bedroom was at the end of the hallway.

It was as tastefully decorated as the rest of the house. The bed, dressers, and nightstands looked like they were made of maple like the floor but were darker in color. Unlike the floors, the furniture looked like it had been distressed. I always wondered why and how furniture manufacturers make new furniture look old and worn. Above the bureau hung a large flat screen television. The remote control was on the nightstand to the left of the bed. Two lamps graced each nightstand.

As I entered the bedroom, I saw a door to the left. I passed through and discovered a large walk-in closet, followed by an en suite bathroom, which was about the same size as the closet. After all the coffee I drank at Perky's, I was ready to use the bathroom and did. After I washed and dried my hands, I looked at the medicine cabinet, which was inset into to the wall to the right of the sink.

The medicine cabinet was larger than any I had seen in the past. When I opened its door, I saw three shelves. Each shelf held bottles of men's colognes and aftershave. Each was a far cry from the Aqua Velva I use after I shave. If Aqua Velva was good enough for my dad, it was good enough for me. Just the same, I had never seen so many in one place, except at CVS or Walgreens. Maybe I needed to up my game. However, these weren't the kinds of men's scents found at local drug stores. Instead, they were high-end brands, with labels from Gucci, Clive Christian, Penhaligon's, Chanel, and others. They revealed that Jamie McIntyre liked to smell nice but, I wondered, for whom. I have always had a theory about men's colognes. This case might put my theory to the test. Time and further investigation should provide an answer.

The vanity top was at least seventy-two inches wide. Because of its width, I was surprised that it contained just one integrated sink and not two. The countertop was made of white marble, with thin black veins running through it. A mirror ran along the width of the vanity and reached the edge of the sink to the ceiling. In each of the drawers below the sink were other sundry items: toothpaste, shaving cream, razor, blades, combs, brushes, jars of pomades and gels, cans of hair spray, and a blow dryer. On the countertop was another square mirrored glass box, which fit over another box of Kleenex, along with a soap dispenser and toothbrush holder that matched the tissue box. White towels in various sizes hung on the racks. Under the sink were two cupboards. When I opened the cupboard door on the left, I discovered a waste basket. It was empty. When I opened the cupboard door on the right, I discovered packages of toilet paper. This room revealed that Jamie McIntyre looked after himself. While most people I know keep their bathrooms clean and tidy, Jamie McIntyre went further. He was fastidious.

I returned to the bedroom looked in each drawer of his highboy and bureau dressers. Nothing seemed out of place. Each drawer contained what you might expect: underwear in one, socks in another, sweaters, T-shirts, and so on. The drawers in the nightstand closest to the window were empty. The two drawers in the nightstand closest to the closet and bathroom held a treasure trove of personal items. One top drawer held a couple of wrist watches, an assortment of cufflinks, tie bars, and some collar stays, which told me Jamie McIntyre was someone who liked to dress well. The bottom drawer held boxes of condoms and surgical jelly, which told me Jamie McIntyre was someone who was sexually active but, again I wondered, with whom? Time and further investigation should provide an answer.

I turned my attention to the closet. There, I would be able to detect the types of clothes and shoes Jamie McIntyre purchased and wore. Further, I would be able to discern whether they were like the ones found on his body when he died. The closet was tidy and well organized, like the other rooms. On one side of the closet were clothes' rods. Shirts hung together on an upper rod with jackets and suits. Jeans hung together on a lower rod with slacks. All garments were arranged by color. On the other side of the closet were shoe shelves. Shoes were also arranged by style and color. Casual shoes were on the bottom shelves, while dress loafers and lace ups were on higher shelves. Toes pointed out rather toward the wall. They shined. On second thought, they gleamed, and even the soles appeared to be well dressed. On the wall at the far end of the closet were tie racks and hooks for belts. All were arranged by color. I didn't see any overcoats, wind breakers, vests, or heavier outerwear. I assumed Jamie McIntyre kept these in a front door closet. I would check on my way out.

For now, I wanted to examine the labels on Jamie McIntyre's shirts and trousers to get a sense of the types of clothes he wore. I also wanted to check his shoe size. First, I looked at the shirt collars. On the shirts with button cuffs, the collars were button down. On the shirts with French cuffs, the collars were either spread or round. On formal shirts, the collars were wing-tip. I found no shirts with straight collars. All shirts—even the casual gingham, striped, and plaid ones—were custom made by one tailor. Next, I looked inside several pairs of trousers. On the inside pocket of each pair, I saw a label that revealed they were custom made by the same tailor. Next, I checked his suits. Again, each one revealed that it had been custom made by the same tailor. I smiled. On my way home, I would visit Jamie McIntyre's tailor. I was confident his tailor would give me even more information than I found here.

Jamie McIntyre's casual shoes revealed that he took a size ten in a medium width. Most of his dress loafers and tie up shoes were made in Italy. They revealed that he took size 43. They also revealed that Jamie McIntyre treated his feet well. He did not scrimp when it came to his shoes.

The importance of my visit to Jamie McIntyre's condominium sunk in. Even though I didn't find his laptop computer, I found out more information than I had thought possible earlier in the day. Much of what I learned matched what his mother told me. Some of what I learned was a complete surprise to me and could come as a surprise to Mrs. McIntyre. I continue to be amazed by how much can be learned about a victim by a visit like this one. Jamie was now more real to me. I started to feel like I knew him. Even better, I had just peeled away other layers of what I knew would be many more layers in the mystery around Jamie's death. What concerned me most was how and when I explained them all to his mother. In all likelihood, I would reveal each layer to her just like I found them: one at a time. However, I also decided that I may have to reveal them in a different order than I found them.

Before I left the condominium unit, I photographed each room from different angles. I also opened each and every drawer and photographed the contents, as well as all the clothes and shoes in the closets. When I finished, I reviewed the camera disk to make sure I captured as much information as possible. On my way down to the lobby, I photographed the hallway and the elevator from outside and inside. Once I reached the lobby of the building, I photographed it in the same way. Joe Lawrence was still on duty. I photographed him too.

While I rechecked the camera disk, I asked Joe if Jamie had many visitors like friends, girlfriends, or coworkers. Joe told me that from time to time, he would see Jamie with a girlfriend. More often, men visited him. Recently, though, Jamie seemed to be more serious about a woman he introduced as Lilly Chin. This was the name of the woman Mrs. McIntyre mentioned to me.

Joe also informed me that while I was upstairs he had accessed guest registration activity on the building's computer. However, he didn't have enough time to segregate the information for Jamie McIntyre's guests, and he didn't know which date range might interest me. So he stopped until he could ask. I was overwhelmed by Joe's initiative and thanked him. He agreed to compile Jamie McIntyre's guest registration data for the last two years. I promised to stop by early next week and pick the list up from Joe. We shook hands. I walked out the main doors to my car and marveled at how much I had learned over the last two and a half hours and how much I had yet to learn. This case had many more layers than I expected.

11

Willis Prescott

When I started out that afternoon, I expected to return to my office, print photographs, and compile notes about my visit to Jamie McIntyre's condominium. However, because of what I found in his closet, I decided to stop by his tailor and find out what information he could share about Jamie. I admit I was surprised when I saw the tailor's labels in Jamie's shirts, trousers, and suits, but I was also relieved to find out that Harper and Hogan custom made his clothes. I knew my former high school classmate, Alex Harper, wouldn't hesitate to share what he knew about Jamie McIntyre. The number of custom-made clothes in Jamie's closet suggested that he must have developed a strong business relationship. Hopefully, Jamie McIntyre had developed his business relationship with Alex Harper. With luck, perhaps Jamie and Alex had developed a friendship as well. I would find out.

It was about fifteen minutes before nine o'clock when I parked my car in the lot adjoining Harper and Hogan. As I entered the store, I could hear the sound of a buzzer in the distance. Within a few seconds, a man walked out to greet me. He was someone I didn't recognize. "May I help you, sir?" I explained that I wanted to see Alex Harper. "He's left for the day, sir. Is there something that I can do for you now?" I went on to explain that I was a friend of Alex's and hoped to speak with him. "Mr. Harper will open the store tomorrow. He'll be in from ten until four, although he often arrives as early as nine or nine thirty. You may be able to speak with him then. May I leave him your name and any message?"

For some unknown reason, I opted not to leave my name or any message. Instead, I decided to wait until I could speak with Alex Harper face-to-face to check his reactions, if any, to my questions about Jamie McIntyre. I don't know why I made this decision, but at the time, my gut instinct told me to keep close counsel. As much as I didn't want to make another trip into the city so soon, I decided to drive in the following morning and try to talk to Alex Harper before he opened his store.

Although it was late and I was tired, I headed back to the office while the images of Jamie McIntyre's condominium were fresh in my mind. The next afternoon, I was due to meet with Mrs. McIntyre again, and I needed to bring myself up to date in order to figure out if and how I was to go on. She was someone who would expect a sound rationale for whatever decision I made about her son's case. That night, I felt a little like Hamlet—to take the case or not to take the case, that was the question.

As I entered my office, I could see the flashes from the red light on my telephone, which meant I had messages. I sat at my desk and pressed the play button on my machine to retrieve them. The machine informed me that I had two new messages and no old messages. The first new message was from someone who wanted to sell me advertisements in some sort of publication that I didn't recognize. I did not record the name or number before I deleted the message. The second message was from Mrs. McIntyre. She called to inform me that she had a conflict and wanted to postpone our discussion until the next day at the same time.

"I know your time is valuable, Mr. Prescott, and my son's case is most important to me, but I was unable to find a substitute for my bridge game tomorrow. I hope you don't think less of me, but the women with whom I play take their bridge game with the utmost seriousness. Right now, these women are all I have. Please call and let me know you have received my message and confirm our new appointment date. I will await your call. You have my number. Thank you."

My mother played bridge. One time, when it was her turn to host her weekly bridge game, I stuck around for a little while just to watch the women play. I wanted to know why my mother was so fascinated by a game of cards. I found out that all the women at the various tables around the room were serious about bridge. They were intense. All played with passion, even my mother. She displayed more passion for her hands at bridge than I had ever seen her display for my late father or for me, so it was no surprise to hear Mrs. McIntyre request a change in her appointment to attend her bridge game. Instead, I was surprised that she had overlooked her bridge game when she scheduled her appointment with me.

Thoughts of my mother led me to thoughts about my late father. He was a fine man. I'm named after him, but everyone called him by his entire first name, Willis. Everyone calls me Will. My father worked hard. He was a good father to me. Yet, I don't remember when he ever displayed emotion or passion for anything; my mother, me, or even football included. Although he sat in front of the family room television to watch football every Sunday, I have no idea if he had a favorite team, much less a favorite player. He never showed any reaction. Often, he watched the game with the sound off. Hours could go by, and I had no idea if either team scored a touchdown.

When he wasn't at work or in front of the television, my father puttered for hours in the garage. I don't know what he did behind the door, except sort screws and straighten nails. After, he would put them in little clear glass jars. He nailed the jar lids to the underside of a shelf in a neat line, then screwed the glass containers onto the lids. My father's garage was organized. As he always reminded my mother and me: "Everything has a place, and everything is in its place." No sooner than he retired from his job, my father died. He dropped dead of a heart attack in his garage. I hope he didn't suffer. I don't think he did. As far as my mother and I knew, he died where he most liked to be. It gave me solace to know my father died where he most liked to spend his time. It gave my mother solace to know that my father died with lots of life insurance, which she could use to spend now she had her own time.

My mother wasted no time after my father's death. After forty-six years of marriage, she was ready for change. She wasn't interested in another man. No, she was interested in new paint, new carpet, and new furniture. Why not? My father didn't like change. In particular, he didn't like any change that cost money. When my father was alive, my mother lacked the freedom to decorate her house and keep it up to date. When she finally had freedom to do so, she started with the living room and moved from room-to-room until she was done. I don't know whether or not she used a professional to guide her. It hadn't matter to me. I no longer lived at home. What did matter was that she was happy, although I confess that I didn't recognize many of the rooms when I visited. Her house became a new home for her, and she didn't have to move to achieve the result. My mother's house doesn't look anything like Jamie McIntyre's condominium or Mrs. McIntyre's house. It may not qualify for a spread in Architectural Digest, but it qualifies for her happiness in my book. It is nice and it looks like her.

I picked up my telephone and dialed Mrs. McIntyre's number. Her telephone rang several times. She did not answer, but her machine answered. As requested, I waited for the beep and left a message to confirm that I received her message and our new appointment date.

After I downloaded the photographs from my camera onto my computer, I decided to print each one. This took time. While I waited, I put my feet up on my desk. I stared at my shoes. They were well-shined, two-toned, leather tasseled Allen Edmonds loafers. But compared to the shoes in Jamie McIntyre's closet, they looked pedestrian. I reflected on my visit to his condominium. I always thought I was a snappy dresser. My former wives thought so too. That day, I discovered that not only my scent and apartment, but my wardrobe paled compared to Jamie McIntyre. Maybe I should buy a better brand of aftershave, move to a nicer apartment, and shop at Harper and Hogan too.

As I thought about changes I could make, I focused on changes to my attire. Why did I spend my money at Macy's or Nordstrom when I could patronize a former classmate? After all, Alex is a friend. I realized now that I should have patronized him rather than the anonymous clerks at department stores who cared more about the sale rather than how I looked. The next day, I planned to speak to Alex about my future wardrobe. Then, I planned to segue into questions about Jamie McIntyre. For now, though, it was time to call it a day and head to my apartment, where I could get a good night's sleep. Maybe in my dreams, I could discover changes I could make before I wound up dead in the place where I spent most of my time—behind a desk.

12

Harper and Hogan

Because of Mrs. McIntyre's postponement, I could spend more time on other aspects of my investigation into her son's death than I planned before I heard last night's telephone message from her. While I still wasn't sure what my decision would be and what I would tell her the following day, so far, my gut told me the police may have missed some important layers to their investigation. The clothes in the paper bag in no way compared to anything that hung in Jamie McIntyre's closet. Similarly, the shoes in the paper bag were a different size, width, and type than any of the shoes on the shelves in his closet. I decided it was time to visit the medical examiner's office and try to account for the clothes and shoes in the bag. Maybe it was as simple as one victim's bag of clothes was mixed up with another bag of victim's clothes. Or, maybe it was as complex as a cover up. Meanwhile, I headed down the highway to Harper and Hogan to meet with Alex Harper before he opened his store.

As I drove from my apartment to Harper and Hogan, I thought about how long I had known Alex Harper—over thirty years. Alex lost his father before I lost mine. I attended his father's funeral, and he attended my father's funeral many years later. While I had left home soon after my graduation from the police academy and married three times,

Alex remained at home to look after his mother. He never married. Alex was a dutiful son. Unlike Alex, I couldn't have remained at home to look after my mother. As it turned out, she was happier on her own.

I don't know why Alex never married. In high school, Alex always dated the prettiest girls. Why wouldn't he? He was an attractive and clean-cut guy. I recall that he had a penchant for cheerleaders, especially blonds. Alex was popular. While he didn't play football, he played basketball and was a high scorer on the court and, if we could believe him, with the girls too. In our senior year, he was prom king. Alex was a great guy. Although we didn't get together often after we graduated from high school, I considered him to be a friend. I believe he felt the same way about me. The next time Mike and I planned to meet for drinks, I promised myself to ask Alex to join us.

Traffic was heavier than the previous day, but it was also rush hour, so I wasn't surprised. It took me thirty-five minutes rather than twenty to reach the lot in front of Harper and Hogan where I parked my car. As expected, the door was locked. The store wasn't due to open for another twenty minutes. However, all the lights were on, so I knew someone was there. I rapped on the glass door. No response. I rapped again. In less than a minute, I saw a figure emerge from the back of the room. As it moved closer, I could tell it was Alex. Because of the sun's reflection on the glass, I wasn't sure if he could tell it was me at the door.

He yelled, "Sorry, we're not open yet."

Then I knew he didn't recognize me. Just the same, I was surprised by his response. I expected a store like his to bend over backwards for a prospective customer. Even if he didn't know who was at the door, I expected him to come to the door and check. For all he knew, it could have been one of his wealthy and long-term customers who wanted to order a couple of suits before he headed off to his own place of business. Now, it was my turn to yell, "Hey, Luther, it's me, Will Prescott."

Alex paused and then hurried to the front door. He unlocked it and welcomed me like a long lost brother. "Will, I'm so sorry. I didn't know it was you at the door. It's unlike me not to open early, but I was in the middle of a project and hoped that I wouldn't be disturbed."

Now, it was my turn to apologize. "Alex, I'm the one who is sorry. When I stopped by last night, I should have left a message."

"You were here last night? Funny, Jeff didn't say anyone had stopped by to see me. Why were you here last night? Why didn't you leave a message with Jeff and why are you here so early?"

Alex's three rapid-fire questions squashed my original plan to play it cool. So much for my idea to ask Alex about a new wardrobe and segue into questions about Jamie McIntyre. Nonetheless, I plowed on. "Alex, I'm here for a couple of reasons. One is personal and the second is professional." I could see Alex's brow furrow. "If you don't mind, Alex, I'd like to pursue the personal one first." I could see Alex's eyebrows rise. "You and I have been friends for more years than I can count, and I can't believe it's taken me this long, but better late than never. If you'll have me, Alex, I'd like to be a customer. Will you help me update my wardrobe?"

I could see Alex's face relax and a smile come to his lips. I had hoped I sounded humble because I was. That morning, I regretted that it had taken me so long to do what I should have done years ago.

Alex didn't disappoint me. "Sure, Will. Thanks. I'd be delighted to help you modernize your wardrobe, although

I'm surprised. I didn't think you needed any help in that department. Even in high school, you were always well dressed. Where did you want to start?"

"Well, when I'm on a case, I'm in and out of my car all day. After a few hours, my shirt and slacks are wrinkled, especially if it's hot. I look like I slept in them. I've heard about these wrinkle-free fabrics. Are they any good?" As I spoke, Alex nodded his head and walked toward a display table that was stacked with shirts.

"Will, what collar size and sleeve length are you?"

Alex bent over. For a moment he disappeared. When he reappeared, he had four shirts between his hands. "These ought to fit you, Will. And, you're right about new fabrics. These are constructed to stay wrinkle-free throughout the day. No need to iron them either. Just take them right out of the dryer and hang them up. You just have to decide if you like any of these colors and patterns. If not, we have others, but I believe these complement your style."

I couldn't argue and had to hand it to my former classmate. Each shirt was perfect. They matched my tastes to a T. However, these fabrics meant I would have to launder them myself rather than drop them off at the cleaners. But, if I looked good and saved a bit of money, they were worth it. "Luther, I'll take all four."

"Well, Will, I don't want to bust your budget this morning. Let's save slacks for your next visit.

If you come later in the day, maybe we can go out for drinks or dinner."

I appreciated Alex's sensitivity to my budget, even though I had been prepared to spend money on slacks too. At the same time, I was happy he suggested drinks and dinner. It would be nice to spend time with him.

"Will, you mentioned you had two reasons for your visit today. What was the other reason?"

As I pulled my wallet out of my back pocket to pay for the shirts, I nodded and said, "I have a case. As part of my investigation, I discovered that the victim bought his clothes from your store. I hope you can shed some light on him for me."

Alex's brow furrowed again. "Sure, Will, I'll try. What's his name?"

"Jamie McIntyre."

Alex stepped away from the counter, threw his shoulders back, stood ram rod straight, and lifted his hands with the palms up. "Jamie McIntyre? Jamie's been dead for months. He was hit by a car. It was really sad. Why on earth would you have questions about him now?"

I explained to Alex that I had been retained to find out more about his death.

"No offence, Will, I know you're a good detective, but I don't understand why anyone would hire you to find out about Jamie's death. Didn't the police investigate? Didn't they charge some woman who was drunk at the time? Has some insurance company hired you so it doesn't have to pay a claim? Is that it, Will? Is that why you're around so you can dig up dirt on some poor guy?"

I shook my head. "Alex, I can't reveal who hired me. That's confidential. But, please trust me. I am not here to dig up dirt. I'm here with the best of intentions. I want to know more about Jamie. Like the police, I would like to close this file too. And, if you can answer a few questions, I can close my file sooner rather than later. So, please, will you help me? Whatever you tell me, I will keep it confidential too."

Alex dropped his shoulders. He seemed to relax. "Okay, Will, I'll tell you what I can, but I gotta tell you, this whole conversation makes me uncomfortable. I knew Jamie all his life. When he was a boy, he came into the store with his father. His dad used to buy all his clothes here. As soon as he was old enough, Jamie started to buy his clothes here too. Jamie's dad and my dad golfed together whenever my father could get away from the store. Heck, my mother still plays bridge with Jamie's mother, Lorna. Jamie's mom and dad went of vacations with my mom and dad. They're like family, for god's sake."

I now understood Alex's defensive reaction, but I still had questions that needed answers. "Based on what I saw in his closet, you did a great job with Jamie's wardrobe. What was he like to work with?"

"I'd like to take credit, but Jeff Cousins was the one who waited on Jamie over the last half dozen years. Jeff was the one who was responsible for Jamie's wardrobe selections. Jamie didn't start to shop here until he started to make big money. That was about five or six years ago. By then, Jamie looked for someone who was younger and could give him more contemporary advice. Jeff was a better fit than me."

"Alex, compared to other customers, was he a big spender?"

"Yeah, I'd have to say that Jamie spent more than the average customer, but we have several who spend more."

"How would you describe Jamie? Was he reserved? Animated? Serious? Devil may care?"

"Will, I know it's become a cliché, but I would have to describe him as someone who worked hard and played hard."

"By played hard, do you mean he was reckless?"

"No, I mean Jamie liked to spend his money on fine foods in fine restaurants, fine wines, nice cars, exotic vacations—those kind of things. He could well afford it. I wouldn't call him reckless. And as far as I know, he didn't do drugs. I'd call Jamie a straight shooter. Jeff told me that they would often go out and enjoy a nice dinner and maybe a show after."

"So Jeff got to know him well?"

"Yeah, they spent a lot of time together. Jamie even took Jeff to Belize on vacation. He paid all Jeff's expenses."

"Wow, so they were really close?"

"For a while. But, unlike Jamie, Jeff doesn't have lots of money. He has just what he makes here. I pay Jeff well, and he makes good commissions, but after his rent and other expenses, he doesn't have the kind of money left over to take the types of vacations Jamie McIntyre took. Jeff told me that he started to back off from Jamie's invitations because he couldn't afford to reciprocate. He said he felt inadequate, and I could tell he felt terrible about it. I have no idea what Jamie thought. In the months before Jamie was killed, I just sensed that their friendship returned to a more professional one than a personal one. Jamie continued to shop here, and Jeff continued to serve him. Based on what I saw, I don't think there were any hard feelings."

"Alex, did Jamie ever come in with a girlfriend? Do you know if he dated much?"

"Yeah, from time to time, I saw a girl come in with him but not often. I met his last girlfriend. I think her name is Lilly. She came in, and Jeff helped her pick out a gift for Jamie. It was either for his birthday or for Christmas. I can't remember, but I do remember she was a real beauty. Apart from that, I don't know much about her or his love life. I don't recall that Jeff ever commented on it either."

As Alex put my new shirts into a bag, I signed the credit card slip to pay for them. We agreed to have dinner in a few weeks after my next visit to the store. Alex promised to pull together a new wardrobe. "Will, I can find you wrinkle-free clothes, but there's nothing I can do about the ones on your forehead and neck. Those wrinkles are there to stay, my friend."

We both laughed. Only good friends can make that kind of crack and get away with it. I left Harper and Hogan happy that morning. I came away with four new shirts, more information about Jamie McIntyre, and my friendship with Alex still intact.

13

Dr. Ortega

As I exited the Harper and Hogan parking lot, it was just before eleven o'clock. I decided to head over to the medical examiner's office and renew my acquaintance with the chief. With luck, Dr. Ortega would introduce me to Dr. Miles Overstreet and I could find out more information about Jamie McIntyre's death.

It took me about ten minutes to reach the medical examiner's offices. I hopped out of the car and approached the double doors. It had been a few years since I had any reason to visit this place. The lapse of time made me forget about the odor that hits and inflames your nostrils as soon as the automatic doors open. It's not a foul odor, like the smell of death which you might expect to find here, but it's not a pleasant one either. It's strong and pungent. My guess is that it's made up of fumes from the various types of disinfectants the office uses to clean its many rooms. Yet, to me it has always smelled more medicinal than fumes from the types of products I use to clean my kitchen and bathroom.

Just inside the foyer, I saw a familiar face behind the reception counter. I wasn't sure if she would remember me. As I approached, she looked up from her desk.

"Well, stranger, long time, no see."

"It's been too long, Heather. How's your husband and kids? I guess they're all grown up now."

"Yep, Jason will graduate from state in June, and Christy is a senior this year. Not sure where she plans to go yet. What brings you here today, Will?"

"I hope to see the chief, and if possible, I hope he'll introduce me to Dr. Overstreet."

"Well, you're a little in luck. Henry is here, but Miles is out on a case. I have no idea when he'll be back. Let me buzz Henry and let him know you're here. Have a seat for a few minutes. Do you want a coffee?"

"No, thanks. I'm coffeed out this morning."

Heather smiled as she dialed Dr. Ortega's extension.

Before I sat on one of the chairs lined up against the front window, I walked over to wall beside Heather's desk. I looked at the photographs of all the medical examiners and office staff. The photographs were framed in black, which stood in stark contrast to the white wall on which they hung. It looked like at least thirty photographs lined the wall in two rows of about fifteen. Each photograph had a plaque below it with the name and title of each person. The photograph of Dr. Ortega was a good one, but he still had all his hair, so I knew it had to be at least fifteen years old. Heather's was good too. I looked down the line of plaques until I found Dr. Overstreet. I don't know when his photograph was taken, but I saw a young man stare back at me. He looked to be in his mid-twenties. I suspected he joined the medical examiner's office when he graduated from medical school. Based on his photograph, Dr. Overstreet was a handsome man. I hoped to meet him some day.

"Dr. Ortega will be with you in a minute. Do you like that photo of me? I can give you an autographed copy if you want one."

"Nah, Heather, I prefer wallet size so I can keep you close to me."

We both laughed out loud. I have always been surprised by the friendliness of everyone in the medical examiner's office. If I had to work with death day in and day out, I don't think I could be as happy as everyone seems to be here. Then again, my ex-wives always wondered why I could be so happy to go to work and face another day of crime. Although I never said anything, after a few years of marriage, crime scenes always seemed like a pleasant diversion to any time spent with them. I guess it's all a state of mind. If you like your job, you're happy and it shows. Why should anyone who works in the medical examiner's office be any different from a guy like me, who loves his job, or millions of others who love their jobs.

All of a sudden, I heard the squeak of soft-soled shoes on the terrazzo floor. I looked up to see Dr. Ortega come toward me with his right hand outstretched.

"Will, how great to see you. I was so surprised when Heather said you were in the lobby. It's been too long." We shook hands. Dr. Ortega invited me to join him in his office. As we walked toward it, he asked, "How's your new business."

I explained to Dr. Ortega that my business was now over seven years old.

"Wow, has it been that long? It seems like yesterday when you were with SPD. Time does fly. What can I do for you today?"

"Dr. Ortega, I have been hired to look into the circumstances of the death of a young man. I hoped I could prevail on you to introduce me to one of your assistant medical examiners who signed off on the death certificate. His name is Dr. Miles Overstreet. I have a few questions to ask him."

"Will, I don't know if Heather told you, but Miles is out on a case this morning. Perhaps I could answer any questions you have. Tell me the deceased's name and I'll pull the file."

"Jamie McIntyre."

"Just a minute."

Dr. Ortega made a few clicks on the keyboard attached to his computer. "Will, please give me a few minutes to look at the file so I can gain some perspective. Then, let's hear your questions, and I'll do my best to answer them. If there are any I can't answer, I'll have Miles call you."

As Dr. Ortega studied his computer screen, I pulled out my pad and pen from my jacket pocket. Although I didn't have many questions, I wanted to be ready to write down Dr. Ortega's answers or any other comments he shared with me.

"Okay, Will. This file looks pretty straightforward. Jamie McIntyre died due to severe trauma as a result of an automobile. What else do you want to know?"

"When an accident victim, like Jamie McIntyre, comes to you for an autopsy, do you also conduct a toxicology test?"

"Yes, Will, we do, especially when death is the result of an accident. In this case, Dr. Overstreet requested one."

"Oh, I didn't see any reference to it on the death certificate."

"Will, that's because toxicology results take about two to three weeks to come back from the lab, so they don't often appear on the death certificate. We try to expedite death certificates so the families of the deceased can get on with funeral arrangements. We don't wait until we have lab reports. Once we they arrive, we turn around and forward them along or any other information like x-rays to the police department."

I asked Dr. Ortega what Jamie's toxicology report revealed. He indicated that it showed Jamie had ingested a modest amount of alcohol before he was killed.

"The report shows Mr. McIntyre's blood alcohol level was .03 percent. It shows no evidence of any medications—legal or illegal." Then, Dr. Ortega chuckled. "Do you want to know about his stomach contents? I've got it all here. Looks like he enjoyed a fabulous dinner."

What is it about people, especially doctors, who work with death? They always seem have macabre senses of humor. Dr. Ortega was no exception.

"No, Dr. Ortega, I'll pass for now. Would it be possible to get a copy of the toxicology report?"

Dr. Ortega made a few more clicks on his keyboard, and within a few seconds, I heard the whir of a printer. Within a few more seconds, Dr. Ortega handed me four pieces of paper. They contained Jamie McIntyre's toxicology report from the lab. I folded the sheets like I would a letter and tucked them in my inside jacket pocket. Without some sort of authorization from either the victim's family or the police department, I was surprised Dr. Ortega gave the report to me. But I wasn't surprised when he asked if I wanted a copy of the coroner's report. It's a public record. Before I could respond, I heard the whir of the printer again. That time, Dr. Ortega handed me eleven pages. These I held in my hand. They were too thick for me to fold and put in my jacket pocket. When I stopped by that morning, I had hoped our former professional relationship would mean something to him, and as it turned out, it did. Just the same, I didn't want to take advantage of it either.

"Will, do you have any other questions for me?"

I decided it was time to broach the subject of the clothes Mrs. McIntyre said were found on Jamie's body. I explained to Dr. Ortega that the clothes returned to the victim's mother did not match the types of clothes that the victim wore. Further, the shoes were not his size. "Is it possible that the office mixed up the clothes and shoes with the clothes from another body?"

Dr. Ortega drew a deep breath and let it out slowly. "Anything is possible, Will, but it's unlikely that such a mix-up took place here. As you know, we are careful to tag every item that comes in with any body. We keep careful records. But, just to be sure, let me check if there were any other bodies here at the same time."

Dr. Ortega returned to his computer keyboard and clicked again on the keys. After a few seconds, he turned away from the screen.

"Will, we had two other bodies when Jamie McIntyre's body was here. Both were female. One was eighty-two and the other was nine. I don't think we would have mixed up their clothes or shoes with Mr. McIntyre's. But, to be sure, let me look at the photographs of Jamie McIntyre that were taken at the scene of the accident."

"You have photographs of the scene too?"

"Yes, of course, Will. Even though the police always take lots of photographs, we take them too. Sometimes we look at the scene differently than the police officers look at the scene. Although, more often than not, we wind up with duplicate views, we find it's an added layer that can help protect the integrity of our investigation. Let's pull up Dr. Overstreet's photographs of the scene."

Once again, I heard the familiar click of Dr. Ortega's computer keyboard keys and the whir of his printer. That time, Dr. Ortega's printer took longer. While we waited, Dr. Ortega asked me about my business. I told him how nice it's been to work on my own timetable and at my own speed. He opined about retirement. He smiled as he said, "I have just two more years, three months and four days to go. Then, my wife and I plan to move away from the city. My ideal place will have lots of scenery. With luck, it will be near a lake so I can fish and near mountains so I can hike. We spend every vacation in search of the ideal retirement spot."

Dr. Ortega handed me copies of the assistant medical examiner's photographs. They were similar to the police photographs in Mrs. McIntyre's file. As expected, the clothes matched. I'm not sure what I thought would be different, except I knew the clothes on the body didn't make sense. I reviewed each photograph to see if I could find shoes. Just like the police photographs, I couldn't see any shoes.

Dr. Ortega must have sensed my disappointment. "This case seems to trouble you, Will. Is there anything I can do to help you find a piece that you may have missed?"

I asked Dr. Ortega if we could go off the record. He nodded his head. I explained how Jamie McIntyre was killed a long way from his home and was found in clothes and shoes that in no way resembled any that he would ever wear. I revealed as much as I could to Dr. Ortega, but as always, I kept some details back.

"Well, Will, the photographs prove the clothes Jamie McIntyre wore the night of the accident match the clothes we found him in. I can't explain why he wore what he wore that night. As to the shoes, I assume Miles found them proximate to the body, catalogued them, bagged them, and placed them with the body while he continued his investigation at the scene. It's possible he made a mistake about the shoes, but I think it's unlikely. After all, who would leave a pair of shoes behind next to a body? Dr. Overstreet wished he had arrived at the scene sooner. As it was, he beat the police and the medivac personnel. He thought he might have been able to try and save Mr. McIntyre. I'm not sure how he could have. Mr. McIntyre's injuries were far too severe for any medical intervention. Miles told me he tried to console the driver of the car, but she was drunk and out of it."

I was surprised to learn this bit of new information about Dr. Overstreet.

"How did Dr. Overstreet arrive on the scene first? Don't the police usually notify the medical examiner's office rather than the other way around?"

Dr. Ortega nodded his head. "Will, it was a weird coincidence. Miles was in the coffee shop near the scene when he heard all the commotion over the accident. When someone ran in and asked for someone to call the police, Miles ran out and tried to render assistance. I am not sure who called the police. I suspect it was someone in the coffee shop."

"Apart from the fact she was drunk, did Dr. Overstreet mention anything else about the driver of the car?"

Dr. Ortega chuckled. "Not much that I can recall, but that she claimed to have seen a large white bunny. Miles and I laughed over that one. I've always heard that drunks see pink elephants, not white bunnies. Will, have you ever seen a pink elephant?"

Now, I chuckled too. "No, Dr. Ortega, I've seen pink flamingos, but I've never a pink elephant, not even at the zoo."

As I spoke, Dr. Ortega's comment about the large white bunny stood out. It was odd. His was the second reference I had heard about the drunk woman's claim about a large white animal. Mike White made a similar reference when we met. Although I had not planned to interview the driver, I made a mental note to reconsider doing so. Maybe she did have something to share. Meanwhile, I stood up from my chair and thanked Dr. Ortega for his expertise and his time.

"Anytime, Will. You are always welcome to stop by. I hope I answered all your questions. Good luck with your case. I'll let Miles know you were here. Perhaps you two will get to meet sometime in the future."

14

Mrs. McIntyre

As I shaved, I wondered if Mrs. McIntyre would serve cookies with coffee at our meeting. I hoped so and decided to eat a smaller breakfast in order to leave room for more than one cookie, just in case she offered them.

Since we last met, I had covered more ground than I had anticipated when I agreed to take a look at Mrs. McIntyre's case. Even though I could account for the clothes in the bag, I couldn't account for the differences in styles and brands. Although they were the right sizes, the clothes didn't match any brands or styles in Jamie's closet. They were just as Mrs. McIntyre said they were—not like any clothes Jamie McIntyre ever wore. The clothes he wore on the night of his death made no sense. I also couldn't account for the shoes, but I knew they did not belong to Jamie McIntyre. Like, the clothes, they were not like any shoes he wore. More importantly, they were not even his size or width. Right now, they were still a mystery. I would have to admit to Mrs. McIntyre I hadn't yet figured out how Jamie McIntyre came to be found in those clothes and how those shoes wound up at the scene.

I put on one of my new wrinkle-free shirts. I chose the white tattersall with red-and-blue check. It looked great with my navy pleated slacks and my pale blue blazer. I decided against a necktie, but I did put a red paisley silk square in my blazer breast pocket. Before I grabbed my keys and headed out the door, I took one last look in the full-length mirror. Yep, I thought, I still had my figure despite my lousy diet. In my opinion, I looked terrific and hoped, when she saw me, Mrs. McIntyre would be as impressed with my results as I was impressed with my appearance. Both my reputation and my new wrinkle-free shirt could be put to the test.

Rather than use McDonald's drive-through window, I went inside to place my order. If I ate and drank while I drove, I was afraid I might drop food or drip coffee on my new shirt. The line was short. Once I made it up to the cashier, I ordered an Egg McMuffin and a coffee.

"Do you want hash browns?"

Although I was sorely tempted, I had already made up my mind and decided against any additional items, just in case Mrs. McIntyre offered cookies or some other treat.

On my way to a table by the window, I picked up a newspaper. It didn't take me long to scan the headlines and to finish my breakfast. I enjoyed the comic section, especially "Pickles," which brought back memories of my previous marriages. For some strange reason, I decided to read my horoscope. It told me to trust my psychic powers and over-come stubborn obstacles. That day's horoscope, like all the others before, offered slim guidance or any words that might cause me to alter my day much less my life. I don't know why I bothered to read them, except for cryptic amusement. I could solve a murder faster than I could make sense of any horoscope. So far, all I got out of it were newsprint ink stains on my fingers.

After a trip to the restroom, I returned to my car, put my clean hands on the wheel, started the engine, and pulled out of the lot. Traffic seemed heavier for this time of day. As a result, I arrived in front of Mrs. McIntyre's house with no time to spare. I ran up her walkway and gave the wrought iron knocker a short bang. Within a few seconds, Mrs. McIntyre opened the door.

"You are always so punctual, Mr. Prescott. Thank you. I appreciate it. So many people are casual about their appointment times. It frustrates me. Please come in."

I stored Mrs. McIntyre's comment at the front of my brain. Although I was seldom if ever late, I would never be late for any appointment with her. Instead, I would take pains to arrive ahead of time.

Mrs. McIntyre led the way, and we sat at the same table and same chairs as before. I was delighted to see both the coffee carafe and a plate with cookies, as well as muffins. No matter how our discussion turned out that morning, I was still in for a least one or two treats over our cups of coffee.

"Please help yourself, Mr. Prescott. I hope you don't have any allergies. The cookies are peanut butter and the muffins are banana and walnut. Coffee?"

I didn't know whether to nod or shake my head. So, I spoke up.

"No, Mrs. McIntyre, I have no allergies. And, please, I would like a cup of coffee." Mrs. McIntyre smiled and poured coffee into two cups.

"I'm sorry I had to change our appointment from yesterday until today. I hope I didn't inconvenience you too much."

"No, Mrs. McIntyre, you didn't. I spent the extra time on your case." "Good. So, what do you have to report?"

I took a few more sips of my coffee and two more bites of the muffin, which was delicious. For a few seconds, I was tempted to embellish my report so I could have more time to eat another muffin and a couple of cookies, but I knew that would be wrong.

Mrs. McIntyre's sensed my hesitation. "Is there something wrong, Mr. Prescott?"

I confessed. "No, Mrs. McIntyre. This muffin is just so tasty, and if your peanut butter cookies are as good as your chocolate chip cookies, I know that I am in for a treat. So, I decided to try and think of way I could stall and find extra time in order to enjoy both."

For the first time, Mrs. McIntyre laughed. She threw her head back and laughed out loud. It was infectious; she made me laugh too. I also noticed that she seemed to relax. For the first time, her brow unfurrowed, her lips unpursed, and her shoulders unfurled.

"Oh, Mr. Prescott, I am happy that you enjoy my cookies and muffins. It's been a long time since anyone sat across from me like this. Thank you. I'll send the rest home with you."

That morning my confession was good not only for my soul but hers too. I'm not sure confession was any good for my waistline.

"Mrs. McIntyre, I covered more ground than expected. First, I met with Detective White to discuss the police file. For the record, Mike White and I are friends. We worked together on the police force for many years." Mrs. McIntyre raised her eyebrows. "Even though Detective White referred me to you, please be assured I would not let our friendship cloud or get in the way of my investigation. Detective White confirmed all that appeared on the copy of the police report you gave me. I learned nothing new from him, except he seemed annoyed I was on the case."

I took another bite of a muffin and a couple more sips of coffee. "Next, I went to your son's condominium. I discovered what you already knew: Jamie would never have bought the clothes that he was found in the night he was killed. I don't know where they came from or why he had them on.

With respect to the shoes, there's no way they belonged to Jamie either. They were too big and too wide for his feet. While the photographs from the scene show the clothes, they do not show the shoes. I don't know where they came from either or why they were given to you."

While I gave my report, Mrs. McIntyre nodded several times. I was surprised she didn't take any notes. Instead, she listened with intent.

"While I was in Jamie's condominium, I found a desk and computer hookup, but I didn't find any equipment like a server, monitor, or laptop. Do you have Jamie's computer equipment or know where it can be found?"

Mrs. McIntyre raised her eyebrows and turned her head. "What? I have no idea. As far as I know, Jamie always carried his computer with him. It should have been at my son's home or in his car. If it wasn't there, maybe it's in his office. I will call later today and ask."

"Please don't call them about the computer Mrs. McIntyre. Instead, would you call his business and ask permission for me to look in Jamie's office?"

"Of course, Mr. Prescott. I will let you know after I speak to them."

"When I checked the labels on the clothes in Jamie's closet, all seemed to come from Harper and Hogan. Because yesterday's appointment was postponed until today, I had all day to investigate. First on my list to visit was Jamie's tailor. I met with Alex Harper."

Mrs. McIntyre smiled as soon as I said Alex's name. "Mrs. McIntyre, I went to high school with Alex Harper."

Mrs. McIntyre's smile grew wider. "Oh, Alex is such as wonderful young man. The Harpers have been friends of our family for years."

"Mrs. McIntyre, I did not tell Alex who had retained me to investigate your son's death. Nonetheless, he told me about your family history and spoke fondly of you, your husband, and Jamie. He also told me how you traveled together."

I could see tension release from Mrs. McIntyre's face and her upper body. Her reaction made it evident to me how much she liked the Harper family and maybe how much she liked the fact I had a relationship with Alex.

"From Alex, I learned Jeff Cousins was the person who most often served your son at Harper and Hogan. Unfortunately, Jeff was not on duty, so I was unable to speak with him. However, based on my discussion with Alex, I knew there was no way your son would have worn the clothes or shoes in the bag."

"Will, why didn't you tell Alex you were retained by me?"

"Mrs. McIntyre, unless a client gives me permission to do otherwise, I keep all relationships confidential. Until I saw the labels on the clothes in Jamie's closet, I had no idea where he bought them, so I had no reason to consider Harper and Hogan or mention my friendship with Alex when I first met you. It was a coincidence. I hope my investigation doesn't affect your relationships with Mrs. Harper or Alex."

"Don't worry, Mr. Prescott. I will tell them about our professional relationship later. For now, it's more important to me to discover how and why my son died the way he did. What else did you find out?"

"After I left Alex, I went over to the medical examiner's office. I hoped to meet Dr. Overstreet, who signed the death certificate. He wasn't there, but I did meet with Dr. Ortega. As it turned out, he answered a lot of questions."

"Really, Mr. Prescott?"

"Yes, Dr. Ortega told me that Dr. Overstreet was on the scene before the police and medivac team. It seems Dr. Overstreet was in the coffee shop within feet of the accident. He responded first to the call for help. I understand that although he wanted to render medical aid, it was too late. There was nothing he could do. However, Dr. Overstreet was able to assess your son's condition at the scene and give details to the officer who arrived a few minutes later. Like the police, the medical examiner's office takes many photographs when they are called out on a case. Your son's case was no exception. Dr. Overstreet took many photographs at the scene of your son's accident. He also transported Jamie's body to the medical examiner's office, completed the autopsy, and signed the death certificate."

I told Mrs. McIntyre that Dr. Ortega showed me Dr. Overstreet's photographs of her son's accident. I tried to account for the shoes. Like the photographs in the police file, the photographs taken in the medical examiner's file showed no shoes. I also told her how Dr. Ortega explained the procedures in the medical examiner's office with respect to a victim's clothes, shoes, and other items. As a result, a mix-up was unlikely. Just the same, Dr. Ortega double checked his files. He found that two other bodies were in the morgue when Jamie arrived. They were females, for which their items were accounted. I decided not to tell Mrs. McIntyre that Dr. Ortega gave me Jamie's toxicology and coroner's office reports. I didn't want to cause her additional concerns until I had a chance to study it.

We finished our second cup of coffee, and I took my first bite of a cookie.

"Mr. Prescott, You have been very thorough in a short period of time. We agreed to assess your investigation after three days. It's now day four."

I couldn't tell by the tone of her voice where she was headed. Did she want to continue the investigation? Or did she want to stop? Most often, I don't care if a client decides to stop an investigation. I do a good job, so I know it isn't personal. Sometimes, clients can't afford to continue investigations. Sometimes, clients learn enough to know that any further investigation is fruitless. Sometimes, but rarely, clients are afraid to know more; their fears about the unknown get in the way. I believed Mrs. McIntyre was a different kind of client. I believed she could afford to find out more, no matter where the investigation led and no matter what I found. Even though I didn't know her well, I also believed Mrs. McIntyre was unafraid.

My thoughts were interrupted by Mrs. McIntyre. "Mr. Prescott, I am impressed by your work so far. It's obvious to me that you have many friends and connections in this city. Doors seem to open for you."

"Thank you, Mrs. McIntyre. I try to be professional at all times. People seem to respond to my demeanor. For example, I forgot to mention my discussions with your son's doorman, Joe Lawrence. He volunteered information to me. Within the next couple of days, he will provide me with a list of everyone who visited your son's condominium during the months before his death. Which brings me to another issue we have not discussed. Where is your son's car? But, please, Mrs. McIntyre, I'm sorry. I got carried away. What did you want to tell me?"

"Mr. Prescott, I would like you to continue your investigation. I have written a check for two thousand dollars as an additional payment for your services. I expect you to account for your services and expenses at the end of each month. Also, I expect you to meet with me each week and provide me with an update on your investigation. Let's meet next week at this time. Meanwhile, I will call my son's office as you requested and ask them to fully cooperate with you. With respect to my son's car, as far as I know, it should be in the garage at his condominium. If it's not there, I hope you will find it parked at his office; otherwise, we have a serious issue. Once you find it, please let me know as soon as possible just so I can put my mind at rest. I hope we don't have to look for a car thief too. A murderer is enough for me to look for right now."

Her last comment drew me back. Although I shared her concerns about the nature of her son's death, I wasn't ready to call it a murder yet. I still had quite a few items on my agenda to pursue before I could call it more than an accident.

As I relished another peanut butter cookie. Mrs. McIntyre stood up. "Please stay seated, Mr. Prescott. I want to wrap some muffins and cookies for you to take with you. Do you have a favorite kind of cookie or muffin?"

"Mrs. McIntyre, I like them all. I'm sure whatever you bake will be delicious."

Mrs. McIntyre placed what was left on the plate in a plastic bag, then added more to it. Then, she sealed the bag and handed it me. "There, Mr. Prescott, these should get you through the next day or two. I'll have more for you next week."

I stood and thanked her. Little did she know that I would polish off everything in that bag on my drive home.

15

File No. 16-12-07MCI

When I Left Mrs. McIntyre's, it was almost noon. After two muffins and three cookies, I wasn't ready for lunch. So, I decided to stop by Jamie's condominium with the hopes that Joe Lawrence would have a copy of the visitor log and could tell me if Jamie McIntyre's car was in the garage. It took me about seven minutes to reach the building and another fifteen minutes to find a place to park, which reminded me why I live in the suburbs rather than the city. Where I live, I can always find a spot for my car.

Joe looked up and smiled as I came through the front doors into the condominium foyer. "How ya doin', Mr. Prescott? Still workin' on that case?"

"Yes, Joe, I am. I stopped by to see if you were able to get me a copy of the visitor log we talked about."

"Mr. Prescott, I'm sorry. When I found time to log in, I found our system ain't workin'. I've reported it, but I don't know when it will be fixed. Them computers drive me nuts. We spend all our time puttin' stuff in them, but when you want to be gettin' stuff out, they don't work. I was able to get you a copy of the garage entry log for the last three months. I don't know if that'll help ya."

Once again, Joe impressed me with his initiative. I was disappointed about the visitor log, but I could wait for it. Meanwhile, the garage report might prove to reveal important information too.

"Thank you, Joe. I really appreciate all your help. Until you told me, I had no idea such reports were even available. You taught me something new."

Joe's chest swelled, and he grinned. I could tell he was happy to help.

"Joe, I know what a pain computers can be. I can review the garage report while we wait for the visitor log. Meanwhile, I hope you can help me with another issue."

"Sure thing, Mr. Prescott. What do ya need?"

"Joe, do you know if Mr. McIntyre's car is in the garage?"

"Which car do you mean, Mr. Prescott?"

I was surprised by Joe's response. I assumed that Jamie McIntyre had one car. Mrs. McIntyre had given me no reason to think otherwise.

"Did Jamie McIntyre have more than one car?"

"Yes, sir. He had two, and they're both beauties. He kept both in the garage, but just one of them is down there right now. Mr. McIntyre used to make me laugh. He called that car his real girlfriend. I could understand why too. It's a real beauty, and it's still all covered up just like usual."

"What kind of car is the one in the garage?"

"It's a red 1963 Corvette Stingray split window coupe. You oughta see it. It'll knock your socks off."

"Joe, before I ask you if I can go down to the garage and take a look at it, what other kind of car did Jamie McIntyre drive?"

"Oh, his other car was real nice too. He just got it before he died. It was a Lexus—one of those SUVs. A real luxury car. I think it was the RX 330 models. It was white but not plain white, like a fridge. No, it was a real pretty color, like a pearl white, with beige leather interior. I swear Mr. McIntyre bought it for the sound system. He played that thing so loud, ya could hear him comin' from the down the block. Mr. McIntyre called it 'my driver.' I have no idea where that Lexus is. Maybe his family has it."

Joe Lawrence was full of surprises.

"Mr. Prescott, if ya follow me, I'll punch in the passcode so you can take an elevator down to the second garage level. When ya get off the elevator, turn to your right, and walk straight ahead. You'll see a beige canvas cover. Underneath is Mr. McIntyre's Corvette. After you're done, I'm afraid you'll have to take the stairs to get back up."

I followed Joe's directions and found the Corvette right away. I lifted the canvas cover at the front driver side corner. Joe was right. This Corvette was a classic, and I was certain it was a rare one too. I have no idea what Jamie McIntyre paid for it, but I suspected it was more than I made in three years, maybe more. I wondered if Mrs. McIntyre knew about the Corvette. She hadn't mentioned it. Then again, she hadn't identified the make and model of his Lexus for me either. For now, I expected to find the Lexus parked at Jamie McIntyre's office. As I put the canvas cover back on the Corvette, I started to wonder about it. If Mrs. McIntyre didn't know about the Corvette, what else didn't she know about her son? But, these speculative thoughts served no purpose now. Until I asked her about the car, they were time wasters.

I saw a door with a sign overhead that said "Exit to lobby," opened it, and discovered stairs. I climbed two floors and found another door with a sign overhead that said "Exit to Lobby." I opened it and found myself near the elevator bank. Joe's desk was on the other side. I walked around and found him seated.

"Thank you, Joe. I'll stop by in a few days for the visitor log. I promise to study the garage report."

"Mr. Prescott, ya don't need to keep stoppin' by. Why don't ya leave me your business card or a telephone number and I'll call ya just as soon as I have it."

"Joe, that would be great, although it might mean I wouldn't see you as often." Joe laughed. I handed him my card. He stared at it for a minute.

"Wow, Mr. Prescott, you really are a private investigator!" He laughed some more. "Are you like that guy Columbo? Or are ya more like Magnum PI?"

Now we both laughed.

"Sometimes, Joe, I'm a little of both."

"No matter, Mr. Prescott. You're always welcome to stop by. I like ya, and I can tell you're a busy man."

"I like you too, Joe, and I'll never be too busy for you. See you soon."

Although Joe said he would call me when he had a copy of the visitor log, I planned to stop by every time I was in the area, regardless. It wasn't because I didn't believe he would call me; I believed he would call. It was because Joe always seemed to reveal more information each time I spoke to him. I knew Joe wasn't coy or disingenuous. He just didn't know what might be important to me. As a result, I had to ask better questions.

16

Mercer and McCarrick

Before I left the city, I decided to make one more stop. So far, my day looked good. Mrs. McIntyre continued to retain me, and Joe Lawrence gave me different yet more information than I expected. I decided to capitalize on my good fortune and stop by the funeral home that handled Jamie McIntyre's arrangements. Perhaps it could shed some light on the clothes and shoes.

Mercer and McCarrick Funeral Home had been in business for as long as I could remember. Although it was one of several funeral homes in the city, it was the oldest and, as far as my family was concerned, the most prestigious. My mother made a call to them within hours of my father's death. They handled my father's funeral just as they handled my grandparents' funerals in the past. This time, I was grateful to visit them for a business reason rather than a sad family occasion.

Mercer and McCarrick now occupied what had been a mansion. It was an impressive house before and even more impressive now. At one time, this area was full of many more large homes. Over the years, the area became commercialized. Many of the homes had been bought by professionals, like lawyers, accountants, and doctors, and at least two were occupied by high-end restaurants. Other homes had been torn down. Mercer and McCarrick bought at least three homes on either side and behind it for additional space. It tore them down. One space was paved over and accommodated at least fifty cars. The space to the west was also paved over to make a large driveway to reach the space at the back. Over the driveway, Mercer and McCarrick constructed a large portico, which was attached to the side of the house. On the space at the back, the funeral home had built an addition to house its vehicles and conduct the part of its business that the public doesn't see.

I climbed the wide front stairs to the covered porch and went through the large front door. I heard the sound of a buzzer when the door opened. Within seconds, a well-dressed man in a gray pin-striped suit stepped into hallway and greeted me.

"May I help you, sir?"

"Yes, my name is Willis Prescott. I'm here this morning on behalf of a client."

"Yes, sir, my name is Leo Mercer."

"You must be the son of Mr. Mercer?" I felt stupid after the words left my mouth. Who else would he be?

"Yes, sir. Did you know my father?"

"Yes, although not well. Our family always uses the services of Mercer and McCarrick."

"Thank you, Mr. Prescott. How may I help your family today?"

"Well, Mr. Mercer, my family doesn't need your services today but I hope you can answer a few questions about your services for someone else. His name was Jamie McIntyre."

Mr. Mercer nodded his head; I didn't detect any concern.

"I have some question about Mr. McIntyre's clothes and shoes." Mercer continued to nod his head.

"Did you pick his body up at the morgue."

"Yes, we did. However, Mr. McIntyre was unclothed. He was wrapped in a white sheet, which is usual practice. So, I don't know how I can answer any questions about his clothes."

I explained to Mr. Mercer that Mrs. McIntyre received a brown paper bag from Mercer and McCarrick, in which she found clothes and a pair of shoes. "We were wondering how these came into your possession?"

"Ah, I now I understand your question. When we pick up a body from the morgue, the medical examiner's office gives us paperwork. Any other items found on or with deceased, such as clothes, shoes, wallet, rings, watches, handbags, eyeglasses, and even dentures, are catalogued by the medical examiner's office and placed in a bag, which is then sealed before it is handed to our personnel. We have no idea what is in each bag unless a family member opens it here and shares it with us."

"Mr. Mercer, is there any way that bags could be mixed up?"

"Most unlikely, Mr. Prescott. We are professionals, and we are careful. I've never known it to happen, but I guess there could be a first time."

"Mr. Mercer, is there any way you could check if you handled the arrangements for another man at the same time you handled arrangements for Jamie McIntyre?"

"Well, Mr. Prescott, your request is an irregular one, but as long as I can maintain client confidentiality and don't have to reveal any names, I'll check our records. One minute, please."

I took a seat on one of the upholstered wing chairs in the hallway. I marveled at the beauty of this place. The ceilings were high. The wallpapers were tasteful. The oak doors were solid with brass handles and hinges. I tried to imagine who lived here before and what type of life they led. Were they happy? When they moved out, did they ever think their home would make way for funerals? I chuckled to myself. Would I give a second thought to how my home might be used when I sold it? Nope. No way. No how. I would take the money and run. I suspect the previous owners saw the changes in their neighborhood and did the same

My thoughts were interrupted by a small cough emitted by Mr. Mercer as he approached me.

"Mr. Prescott, I have checked our records. During the six days around Mr. McIntyre's funeral, three days before and three days after, we had four other funerals."

Wow, I thought, business is good at Mercer and McCarrick.

"Those four funerals were for females. Two of the four were elderly. A third was in her forties and the fourth was for a nine-month-old infant. Would the clothes and shoes in question be ones that any of these decedents would wear?"

"No, Mr. Mercer, I don't think any of them are candidates. I want to thank you for your assistance. I appreciate it."

"You're most welcome, Mr. Prescott. Have a good day."

On some level, I suspected I would hit another dead end with respect to who might own the clothes and shoes. Just the same, I had hoped to solve this riddle today. I realized now that the clothes and shoes were part of a much bigger puzzle. I also realized it might be a tougher case to solve than I had thought. All I could do was peel the onion back one layer at a time until I got to its core and solved this puzzle.

17

File No. 16-12-07MCI

Overnight, I thought about my visit to the funeral home. I realized it hadn't been a bust after all. I could now check the funeral home off my list of places I was required to visit in order to learn more about Jamie McIntyre's clothes and his death. And, on balance, the rest of the previous day had gone well. At each stop of my investigation, I peeled away another layer of the onion and learned new details. For a private investigator, like me, information is the name of the game.

Until Mrs. McIntyre received approval from her son's office, I wasn't free to stop by and ask questions. However, I was free to check to see if his car was parked in the office lot. I was tempted to drive by and look. First, though, I needed to find out the tag number on his SUV. I didn't know how many white Lexus SUVs might be around. When I had a chance to scan the lot, I needed to be be certain I found the correct car in order to make my visit fruitful. I decided to get the tag number that morning while I waited for Mrs. McIntyre's call. I could scan the lot when I met with office staff. A small delay wouldn't make much difference at this stage in the investigation.

Meanwhile, I looked at the other items on my agenda to figure out who I needed to meet with next. Two names stood out. One name on my list was Monique Lewis, who was the driver of the car. She ran over Jamie McIntyre not once but twice—forward and backward. The other name on my list was Lilly Chin. As far as I knew, she was the last known girlfriend of Jamie McIntyre. My gut told me it was premature to meet with the driver until I compiled more information. However, I couldn't come up with a reason not to meet with Jamie's girlfriend.

I pulled out Mrs. McIntyre's files and found two telephone numbers for Lilly Chin. I assumed one number was for her home telephone, and the other number was either for her office telephone or mobile telephone. I picked up my receiver and pushed buttons for the first number. I hit pay dirt: Lilly Chin answered on the second ring. While she was hesitant to meet with me, I managed to convince her to set up a time when she finished work. Her workday ended at three. We agreed to meet in the Sheraton Hotel's bar, which she said was near her office at three thirty. Now I had a reason to drive to the city and I could look for Jamie McIntyre's car in his business lot.

Through my contact at the Department of Motor Vehicles, Gwennie Bedford, I was able to get Jamie McIntyre's plate numbers for both the Lexus and the Corvette in a matter of minutes. Because I am suspicious by nature, I asked for both tag numbers. I wanted to eliminate any possibility the plates on these cars were interchanged. Over the years, I learned the lengths to which owners who default on their loans and thieves will go to keep their cars. Most often, they replace their tags with ones they steal from similar vehicles in order to avoid detection by skip tracers and police. Their ploys work for a while, but we always catch them in the end.

Before I called the Department of Motor Vehicles, I should have gone through the list of cars Joe Lawrence had given me. I also should have reviewed the toxicology and coroner's reports Dr. Ortega gave me two days before. However, the issue of Jamie McIntyre's car gnawed away at me. I couldn't sit still to read any reports no matter how important they were until I checked the lot for that Lexus. I needed to know if it was there.

As I spoke with Gwennie Bedford, I wrote down the information for the file. She told me that Jamie McIntyre had vanity plates for each of his cars. The plate for the Corvette was JAMC 001 and the plate for the Lexus was JAMC 002. Although both were easy plates to remember, I had to remember which plate was assigned to which car. It would be easy to mix them up. I had forgotten to look at the plate on Jamie's Corvette when I saw it in the garage. I reminded myself to do so next visit. For now, I decided to rely on an old tried-and-true method to avoid any confusion as I tried to scan vehicles in the lot. Number "1" was closer to the letter *c,* so I could remember that JAMC 001 belonged to the Corvette. That way, I knew I should look out for a white Lexus with a plate that ended in the number "2."

I returned a few telephone calls from insurance companies and picked up two new cases. They wanted me to find beneficiaries who were named on life insurance policies. The insurance companies couldn't find them. I loved these types of cases. At first, beneficiaries were sad to learn that someone in their life had died, but their sadness always gave way to happiness when they found out they were due for an unexpected windfall. And, me, well I was happy to be paid by a reliable client for my efforts. By the time I ended these calls, I was hungry, which meant it was time for lunch.

Next to food from McDonald's and Perky's, I like Chinese food. Between my office and downtown Sacramento, I remembered a great place called China Star. It offered a lunchtime buffet. If I left the office now, the lineup wouldn't be too long and I could enjoy a feast of all my favorites. The thought of wonton soup, fried rice, Szechuan chicken, Kung Pao shrimp, pork chow mein, and Hunan beef made my mouth water. I have no idea if any of the dishes were authentic Chinese dishes; I didn't care. They tasted good. Even better, I could try as many as I wanted and as often as I wanted until I was full. I liked to wash my meal down with hot tea. Anywhere else, I drank Coca Cola, but when I go to China Star, I order hot tea. I think it may be green tea. However, on days when I ate Chinese for lunch, I brought a bottle of water with me to place in my car's cupholder. The salt in the Chinese food dishes makes me thirsty.

May, the hostess, greeted me as I came through the black wooden door.

"Mr. Prescott, how nice to see you again. Table for one or two?"

"Just for one today, thanks, May."

I followed May to a table by the window, which I preferred. While I was seated a little further away from the buffet line, the rest of the restaurant tended to be dark. I liked it brighter, and I could look outside while I ate.

"Tea, Mr. Prescott?" "Yes, please, May." "Okay, and soup?"

"Yes, please, May, wonton."

"Yes, sir. Your server will bring your tea and soup in a few minutes. Go ahead and help yourself to the buffet."

She left an order ticket on the table, along with a rolled napkin filled with silverware. I unrolled the napkins and placed the fork to my left and the knife to my right. As I stood, I placed the napkin on the back of my chair to let other diners know that it was taken and walked to the buffet.

Two people, a man and a woman, were in front of me as I took a dinner plate from a tall stack.

Before me was a steam table that held what seemed to be an endless line of stainless steel trays, each of which contained a different type of food. I found it difficult to know what to select first. I decided to go with my favorites, just in case I ran out of room . . . in my stomach not on my plate. I could always get another plate of food. After I selected a spring roll and covered it with plum sauce, it didn't take long for me to cover my plate with other goodies. I returned to my table and found my soup and tea before me. Life was good. I picked up the white china soup spoon and picked out a noodle. The wonton noodles were soft and filled with minced pork. The broth was hot and savory. I finished the soup in a matter of seconds. I pushed the bowl away and poured myself tea into a delicate vessel. It looked more like an egg cup than any of the cups from which I drink my coffee. I dug into the heap of food on my plate. Between bites, I took a sip of tea. I was in heaven. By the faces of diners around me, they were too.

I stared out the window as I ate my meal and focused on cars parked outside and cars that drove by. Within fifteen minutes or less, I discovered just how many Lexus were on the road. I was amazed. Before I knew Jamie McIntyre owned one, I don't believe I had ever given a Lexus a second thought. My vehicle brand of choice has always been Ford. As a detective, I spend a lot of time in my car—sometimes hours in one spot when I can't run my air conditioner or heater. My car has to be comfortable. No leather seats for me. I prefer cloth seats; they're cooler in summer and warmer in winter. Just the same, I wondered what was so special about Lexus that attracted so many drivers like Jamie McIntyre. And I wondered why anyone would buy a white car rather than a black one. In my opinion, white cars were plain and ho hum, while black cars were attractive and dignified.

My thoughts about automobile brands and interiors were interrupted. A server came by to check on me. From time to time, a server came to pick up my empty soup bowl or my plate. Every time I looked up, I saw a different server. I didn't recognize any of them. I went through two more plates of food. Each one was as delicious as the first. I handed my credit card to last server who stopped by. She took it and the ticket on the table to the front desk where May processed my check. The server returned with my card and two credit card charge slips. After I included a tip and signed one copy, I left it behind with the pen on the table. I saved the other copy for my expense report and placed it in my wallet, along with my credit card. I was now ready to take on any project and even a search for a white Lexus in an office lot. Before I stood up, I wiped my face one last time with my napkin. When I smoothed my shirt, I discovered a spot just below the third button. It was dark and round. Based on its color, I knew it wasn't sweet and sour sauce. So, it was either tea or soy sauce. If I couldn't blot it out with cold water in restroom, I would have to wear a necktie to cover it up. That prospect gave me pause. But I decided not to let it interfere with my outlook. A necktie was small price to pay for a great meal, and I knew I wouldn't need the tie until I met with Miss Chin.

The drive from China Star to Jamie McIntyre's offices took longer than I expected because I seemed to hit every red light on the way. As I pulled in the lot, I noticed just a few empty spaces. I decided to park my car in one and walk around the lot rather than drive. Although my walk might attract attention, I was prepared to take the risk. I grabbed my camera and headed toward the furthest corner of the lot where I started to walk up and down each aisle.

In the first aisle of parked cars, I discovered three Lexus, but each was a different model and each was a different color than Jamie McIntyre's vehicle. In the next aisle, I was surprised to find no Lexus. The third aisle produced one Lexus, but it was a cranberry red color. The fourth produced no Lexus. I hit pay dirt in the fifth aisle. I spotted two white Lexus, and they were parked side by side. How convenient. As I walked toward them, I observed that one was brighter than the other. It was so clean I was almost blinded by the sunlight that bounced off it. The body and the windshield of other was thick with dust as if it had sat in the lot for a long time.

My heart beat a little faster as I came closer to the dirty car. Had Jamie McIntyre's car been parked here since his death? Perhaps that's why it was covered in dust. Once I was behind both vehicles, I could see the plates. To my dismay, neither plate matched the ones registered to Jamie McIntyre for either of his cars. My shoulders slumped. I was disappointed. Nonetheless, I decided to take a series of photographs of both cars and their attendant tags, although I took more photographs of the dusty one.

The last aisle yielded no Lexus at all. Just to be sure I hadn't missed a car, I retraced my steps back to the corner where I had started my search. I found no other Lexus. What I did find was a compact car that looked out of place. It was a red Nissan, and it was old, dented, and rusty. All the other vehicles were larger, newer, and in mint condition. These cars told me that employees who worked here did well, except for one poor schnook. For a silly second, I wondered what he or she did for the firm. For kicks, I decided to take a photograph of the Nissan. When I met with the office staff, I might ask about it. For now, though, my focus was on Jamie McIntyre's Lexus. Where was his car? If it wasn't in the condo garage and it wasn't here, where had he left it? Maybe his girlfriend could shed some light on this mystery.

18

Lilly Chin

I arrived at the Sheraton with about ten minutes to spare before I was due to meet with Jamie McIntyre's last girlfriend, Lilly Chin. As I entered the restroom, I pulled out my necktie from my jacket's right-hand pocket. I lifted my shirt collar, did up the neck button, placed my necktie around my shirt neck, tied a Windsor knot, pulled my shirt collar back down, and smoothed my tie on the front of my shirt—now no one could see the spot on my shirt. I still couldn't identify its source. I combed my hair and washed my hands. In my opinion, I looked extraordinary for a guy who had spent most of the day focused on ordinary tasks.

Except for the bartender, the bar area was empty. Unlike many bars, which are dark, this one was bright. It was at street level and surrounded by full-length windows. I grabbed a table at the far end and sat on one of the two bar stools. Before the bartender could come and take my order, I saw a woman enter and look around. She was tall. She looked elegant. She was blond. She was beautiful. If I wasn't here to meet Lilly Chin, I might have made a move. But that afternoon was about business not pleasure. I was surprised and overjoyed when the woman walked toward me. Maybe I hadn't lost my charisma after all.

"Are you Mr. Prescott?"

I stood and replied, "Yes, I am."

"Hi, I'm Lilly Chin." We shook hands.

"Nice to meet you Miss Chin. May I order you a beverage, glass of wine, cocktail?"

She nodded. We took our seats as I motioned to the bartender to come over.

"Mr. Prescott, by your expression you seemed surprised by me." "I admit I was surprised when you approached me."

"Did you expect to meet someone who looked Asian?"

"Yes, Miss Chin. I confess. I did expect you to be Asian."

Miss Chin laughed. She was even more beautiful than I first thought.

"Did you expect someone with dark straight hair and almond eyes?"

I tried to bury my head in my shoulders but knew it wouldn't work. Miss Chin was gracious, even though I had made an incorrect assumption.

"Because of my last name, people often assume I'm Asian. While Chin is an Asian name, it is also an English name. My parents were born in England and are of Anglo Saxon descent. They tell me that our last name is a derivative of the last name Chinn. Many last names in the United Kingdom are based different origins. In Scotland, surnames, like 'MacDonald' are clan names. In England, surnames can be based on places. For example, the last name 'Oxford' comes from Oxfordshire. Sometimes, last names are based on trades, such as 'Plumber,' which you might think comes from people who fix pipes in bathrooms, but it actually comes from people who sold plumes or feathers. We believe our last name came about because we had distinctive chins."

By the promptness, completeness, and self-assuredness of her response, I knew Lilly Chin had offered this explanation countless times before, yet she seemed to take no offence. Instead, she chuckled as she delivered this history lesson in last names. She put me at ease to the extent I was tempted to ask her if she knew the origin of my last name, but I decided against it. I felt relieved and could understand why Jamie McIntyre dated her. Miss Chin was remarkable. Although I felt unremarkable in her presence, she made me feel special.

The bartender lumbered over. Miss Chin ordered a glass of Sauvignon blanc, and I ordered a Budweiser. If relationships were based on what people ordered to drink, I guessed that our drink orders revealed a relationship between us was unlikely. Hers said high class and mine said low class. But I could dream. Wow, I thought, this was a first. I couldn't believe how intimated I was by her. No woman had ever done that to me before. I finally figured out what the lyrics meant on the old Ella Fitzgerald record my parents played over and over again. I was bewitched, bothered, and bewildered.

While we waited to be served, we made small talk. Miss Chin explained that she is a nurse in the Sutter General Hospital emergency room or "emerg" as she called it. At that time, her shift was from seven in the morning until three in the afternoon, but her shifts change with some frequency. Night shifts are tough because they make it difficult for her to date. I commiserated and told her how police work had ruined two of my three marriages. She didn't bat an eye. At that moment, I thought perhaps I stood a chance with her after all. Miss Chin went on to tell me she was born and raised in southeast England, near Canterbury. Once she became a registered nurse, she decided it was time to leave home and explore the world.

First stop, she said, on her worldwide adventure was the United States. Miss Chin explained she had relatives who could sponsor her visa. They provided her a temporary place to stay and directed her to jobs, which, for nurses, were plentiful.

"If this is your first stop, where do you plan to venture next?"

"I'm not sure, Mr. Prescott. Perhaps, I'll just venture to another part of the U.S. Unlike England, this country is so vast and has so many different and unusual areas. My next stop might be Colorado. The mountains are so beautiful. Imagine, Mr. Prescott, if you could wake up every morning and see them so close. So majestic. So rugged."

I had to admit she painted a nice picture. Our drinks arrived.

"Cheers! Mr. Prescott."

"Please call me Will."

"Thank you, if you will call me Lilly in return."

We tapped glasses. With those formalities and our small talk out of the way, I could try to get down to business, although I admit Lilly made it tough. Her deep blue eyes, long eyelashes, perfect patrician nose, rounded full lips, flawless peach-colored complexion, and long blond hair got in my way. I couldn't take my eyes off her. She had made me tongue-tied, which was not good for a private investigator who was supposed to be on the job.

"As I mentioned on the telephone, I have been retained to investigate the death of Jamie McIntyre."

"I thought it was an accident."

"The police department declared his death an accident, but the party who hired me is not so sure. My job is to find out one way or the other."

Again, Lilly Chin didn't bat an eye. She focused on me. She was intent. I could tell she was curious about what I had to say.

"Lilly, how long did you know Jamie McIntyre?"

"Oh, I believe I met him just over eighteen months ago, but we didn't start to date until about three or four months before his death."

"Really. How did you meet?"

"We met at a hospital fundraiser of all things. It was a dinner, dance, and auction. I accompanied one of the doctors from the hospital who didn't want to go alone. There was nothing between the doctor and me. I was just his date for the evening. Anyway, Jamie McIntyre and his company were prominent sponsors of the event. He was one of the hospital dignitaries who formed a line and greeted everyone as they entered. I was briefly introduced to him at the time, but it was cursory. When the cocktail party ended and we took our seats for the dinner, I found myself seated next to Jamie. That's when I got to know him better. But, again, our conversation was what you would expect at any dinner where about three hundred people are thrown together to raise money."

"You sound like you don't enjoy those kinds of events."

"I don't. Perhaps it's because I don't run in those circles. I have a limited budget, which doesn't allow me to attend charity balls unless I am invited as a guest."

I was relieved to learn she was humble.

"After the dinner and auction were over, the dance started. My date didn't ask me to dance, but Jamie did. I got to know him better on the dance floor. By the way, he was a great dancer. As the night came to an end, Jamie handed me one of his business cards and asked me to call him. I thought it was a bit odd. It's more customary for men to ask me for my telephone number and ask if it's okay to call me rather than have me call them."

Wow, I couldn't believe Jamie McIntyre was so cavalier with this woman. His ego was more intact than mine.

"So, Lilly, when did you call him?"

"Well, I intended to call him soon after the event, but I couldn't remember where I put his business card. Most often, I would put a card like his in my wallet. However, that night, I carried a small clutch purse, which wasn't large enough to hold my wallet or much else for that matter. So, it wasn't until a few months later I found it tucked away in that bag. Then, it took me a few weeks to muster courage to call Jamie. I was afraid he wouldn't remember me."

I couldn't imagine any red-blooded man could forget this woman. She was someone I would always remember no matter how our meeting turned out.

"Anyway, I called Jamie at his office. He wasn't there, so I decided to leave a message for him. In a few days, he returned my call. To my surprise, he remembered me and wondered why I had taken so long to reach out to him. After I explained what happened, he laughed and invited me out to dinner. Jamie McIntyre was a true gentleman. He was thoughtful. My hospital schedule didn't bother him because, as he told me early on, his business travel schedule was hectic. Sometimes, he had to break dates, but he always made up for it with flowers or a gift that he picked up for me on his travels. He had excellent taste. I miss him. I believe we were on the brink of a serious relationship despite our five-year difference in age. Unfortunately, he died before we became intimate."

When Lilly dropped those last two sentences, she made my head spin. Lilly had just alluded to a five-year age gap that I couldn't reconcile and seemed to have suggested no sexual relationship with Jamie McIntyre. I had to think of a polite way to ask about both issues. At the same time, I didn't want to offend this beautiful woman, but I had a job to do. This onion had so many layers. Every time I peeled one away, more revealed themselves.

"So, you were five years younger than Jamie?"

"No, silly, I was five years older, but Jamie didn't care."

Now, I had to plunge in and ask the more difficult question. "What did you mean by 'intimate'?"

"What do you think I meant? Are you a prude, Will Prescott?"

At first, I thought I detected a note of anger in her voice. But as she spoke further, I could tell she was honest, straightforward, and somewhat playful.

"Will, we hadn't gone to bed together. We hadn't enjoyed sex. Our relationship seemed on the brink of that kind of intimacy, but as I told you, Jamie was a gentleman. Sometimes, I wished that he hadn't been such a gentleman. I wanted to be close to him. I wanted to share his bed."

Yes, she was sincere, and I could tell her thoughts of what might have been with Jamie conjured up grief and regret. She grew quiet. I regretted that I had to ask her these and any more questions. I wished I could have been more solicitous. All I could mutter in response was "I understand." After a short pause, I returned to business. "If you don't mind, I am interested to know if you have anything more you would like to tell me about Jamie?"

"What do you mean?"

"Well, before I clarify, please let me ask if you would care for another glass of wine or something else? Perhaps I could order some hors d'oeuvres?"

Lilly smiled. "Yes another glass of wine would be lovely and something to nibble on would be nice too. Thank you, Will."

I was grateful both for her smile and her indulgence. No one likes to be questioned about a former relationship, especially by a stranger. In our haste to try and solve a crime, police, no matter their rank, and investigators, like me, often forget our questions can be intrusive and insensitive. As a result, we come across as unsympathetic. Our jobs can get in the way of our humanity. That day, I worked hard to overcome this career shortfall. Lilly Chin was someone I wanted to know better.

The hotel bar didn't offer much in the way of hors d'oeuvres. As I scanned the menu, I tried to order items we could both enjoy. Chicken wings were out because they would be too messy. In as much as Lilly expressed no preference, I settled on fried shrimp, quesadillas, and nacho chips with chile con queso and salsa dips. While we waited for our drinks and appetizers, Lilly excused herself for a minute or two in order to check her pager for any messages. When she was done, she looked up and surprised me by what she said.

"Will, I dreaded this afternoon. I was afraid to confront my memories of Jamie. But, you are an easy man to talk to. I have enjoyed my afternoon with you. Perhaps we can get together again when this business about Jamie is behind you."

I almost fell off my chair. No matter what I uncovered on this case, I knew I had discovered the woman of my dreams. My biggest job now was not to blow it.

"Thank you, Lilly. You are most kind. I have enjoyed this afternoon too, and I apologize if I have made you uncomfortable. That was not my goal. My focus this afternoon and in the days ahead is to find more about the nature of Jamie's death. I would like to get together with you again. But I won't give you one of my business cards and ask you to call me. Instead, I promise to call you."

She laughed out loud. Hers is a pretty laugh if a laugh can be pretty, but I think everything about Lilly Chin is pretty.

We sipped our drinks, snacked on hors d'oeuvres, and talked about Jamie, as well as a host of other things over the next several hours. I couldn't believe it when I looked at my watch. It was eight o'clock.

"Lilly, I am not sure what I expected when I made the appointment with you, but this meeting has been a treat. Thank you."

"It's been a treat for me too, Will. I have to be at work by seven tomorrow morning, so I should be on my way."

"May I drive you home?"

"No, thanks, Will. I just live a block away. Tonight's a nice night. I'd like to walk home. I hope there'll be other chances for you to drive me home."

I stood as she rose and came around to the table to hold Lilly's chair and help her put on her coat. Just before she turned to walk away, she gave me a quick kiss on my cheek.

"Goodbye, Will. I hope to see you soon."

I was grateful that the bar stool was beside me. When she kissed me, I felt my knees buckle. As I tried to keep my balance, I remained silent as I watched her walk out the door. When Lilly passed by the bar windows and gave me a wave, I smiled back like I had never smiled before.

19

Mrs. McIntyre

Most days, when my alarm clock buzzes, I reach over, shut it off, and jump out of bed. Not that day. That morning, when I heard the alarm, I wanted to roll over and continue my dreams about Lilly. Last night, I enjoyed my best sleep in ages, which I knew was due to my evening with her. However, my professional responsibilities called. I had to put any dreams about Lilly on hold. In several of hours, I was due to meet with Mrs. McIntyre and give her my weekly progress report. It was time for me to get up. While I wondered what she would serve with coffee at our meeting, I threw off the covers, sat up, put my feet on the floor, stood up, and stretched my arms high above my head—this was the extent of my daily exercise.

I was about ten days into this case. The past week had flown by. While I showered and shaved, I reviewed my activities and compiled a mental checklist of what that I accomplished over seven days. It was a lot. However, I still hadn't reconciled the mystery of the clothes and shoes Jamie was found in the night he died. The medical examiner's office and the funeral home offered no solutions to the mystery, and I could think of no other source for an answer except Jamie's workplace. I believed his office was a long shot unless I discovered Jamie kept clothes and shoes at his office.

However, I suspected he was like me. All I kept at my office was a spare shirt and tie. I didn't keep extra shoes and slacks, and I assumed that was all he kept too.

As I continued to ready myself for the day, my mind wandered away from the case to Lilly. She was the girl of my dreams—literally. I wondered if I could measure up to Jamie McIntyre in Lilly's eyes. I wasn't rich like him, but I did earn a decent income and could show a girl a good time. Unlike Jamie, I had been married before—three times—but that was only because I hadn't found the right girl. In other ways, I was like Jamie McIntyre. I'm a snappy dresser, and in time, my wardrobe will come from Harper and Hogan just like his. Even though I was older than Jamie and had a few gray hairs to show for it, my figure was still youthful for a guy my age. And, I could be a gentleman too, although I'm not sure I could be as much of a gentleman as Jamie was to Lilly.

The sting of the aftershave on my cheeks brought me back to reality and the fact that Mrs. McIntyre might have to accept that her son's death was an accident, not a murder. So far, Jamie McIntyre's case hinged on those clothes and those shoes. It was possible they could remain a mystery. I wasn't ready to have that discussion with Mrs. McIntyre until I met with Jamie's coworkers, checked out his laptop, found his car, looked at his bank statements, and reviewed the visitor list from his condominium. And, I still had the toxicology and coroner's reports to read, as well the photos to upload and review. On one hand, I still had a long list of things to do, but on the other hand, I didn't want to give Mrs. McIntyre hope if I couldn't find any. I had to be candid with her even if it meant I had to give up her fees.

I buttoned up my new blue button-down shirt and tucked the tails into my tan slacks. I decided to wear my navy blue blazer but no necktie. However, just in case I spilled something on my shirt again, I pull a striped tie off the rack and put it in my jacket pocket.

At last, I was ready to meet with Mrs. McIntyre right after I visited my office and enjoyed my favorite breakfast: an Egg McMuffin and a large black coffee.

While I sipped my coffee, I saw the light on my telephone flash. I had one message. It was from Mrs. McIntyre. She called to confirm our appointment. While I ate my Egg McMuffin, I uploaded the photographs from my camera onto my computer, checked to make sure they were all there, reformatted the disk, and put it back into my camera. After I met with Mrs. McIntyre, I planned to return to my office and review all the photograph, the toxicology and coroner's reports, and Jamie's condominium garage entry list. That garage list also served as a reminder to stop by the condominium to see if Joe Lawrence had obtained a copy of the visitor list.

My drive into the city was uneventful. I arrived in front of Mrs. McIntyre's home on time. As I looked in the rear-view mirror to make sure I didn't have anything stuck between my teeth and my hair was still in place, I wondered what Mrs. McIntyre would serve today. Her cookies were my favorites.

Just as she had done for all my previous visits, Mrs. McIntyre led me from the front door to her kitchen, where we sat on the same chairs. She poured me a cup of coffee and offered me not one but three types of cookies. It was as if she had read my mind. Before me was a small silver tray with shortbread, chocolate chip, and oatmeal-raisin cookies.

"Please help yourself, Mr. Prescott."

"Oh, Mrs. McIntyre, you've made all my favorites. I don't know which one to choose first."

She grinned. "I'm so happy that you like them. Now that I have no one besides myself for whom to cook or bake, it gives me great pleasure to see you eat them."

"Mrs. McIntyre, believe me when I say you are the best baker ever, but please, please don't tell my mother."

She chuckled and shrugged her shoulders, like she was a co-conspirator in a cookie contest.

As I munched on my second cookie, Mrs. McIntyre got down to business. "What do you have to report to me this week, Mr. Prescott?"

"Well, Mrs. McIntyre, I visited the funeral home. Mr. Mercer could offer no explanation about the clothes and the shoes. He insisted that whatever clothes or shoes accompanied your son to the funeral home were catalogued by the medical examiner's office and came to them in a sealed bag.Further, there was no chance of a mix-up with any other arrangements before or after Jamie entered Mercer and McCarrick. For now, I've hit a dead end with respect to the clothes and shoes.

"When I met with Joe Lawrence at your son's condominium, he told me Jamie owned two cars. Through the Department of Motor Vehicles, I obtained the license plate numbers for both. Did you know Jamie owned two cars, a red Corvette and a white Lexus? I saw his red Corvette parked in his condominium garage but no Lexus. While I planned to wait until I met with Jamie's coworkers, I decided to scout his office lot to see if his white Lexus was parked there. It wasn't. Do you have any other ideas as to where it might be?"

I could tell by the look on Mrs. McIntyre's face that the news about her son's cars unnerved her. "Mr. Prescott, I'm sorry but I didn't know Jamie owned a Corvette. It must have been a recent acquisition. I just knew about his white Lexus and assumed it would be parked on his office lot. If it's not there or in his condominium garage, I have no idea where else it might be. On top of the mystery of the clothes and shoes, his cars present a new mystery and a new worry for me."

"Mrs. McIntyre, have you been able to contact Jamie's office and arrange a time for me to visit? In addition to questions I have for his coworkers about his car and other issues, I hope to find his laptop in his office."

"Yes, Mr. Prescott, Jamie's vice president, John MacKay, will be happy to meet with you tomorrow at two o'clock. John has assured me that you will receive the company's full cooperation."

"Thank you, Mrs. McIntyre. I also met with Lilly Chin."

Mrs. McIntyre's raised her eyebrows. I couldn't tell by the look on her face if she thought this was a good thing or a bad thing.

"What did you think of Miss Chin?"

"I like her. She's very beautiful, she's intelligent, she's a great conversationalist, and I can understand why Jamie's dated her."

"I can tell she charmed you like she did my son."

Now it was my turn to raise my eyebrows.

"Please forgive me, Mr. Prescott. I'm sure Miss Chin is a lovely woman. Like all mothers, I never thought any woman was good enough for my son. It's silly of me, but I couldn't help myself. I'm sure your mother feels the same way about you. Did Miss Chin offer any insights about Jamie's death?"

"No, Mrs. McIntyre, she didn't, but she did say that Jamie was a perfect gentleman. I think that it is a great tribute to you as much as it is to Jamie. It speaks to how well you raised him."

Mrs. McIntyre nodded. "Thank you, Mr. Prescott. Mr. McIntyre and I did our best to instill our son with good values. It's nice to hear that we succeeded. Where do we go from here?"

"Tomorrow, I will visit Jamie's office. After I leave you, I will stop by Jamie's condominium and check if a copy of the visitors' log is available. Later this week, I will review the toxicology and coroner's reports from the medical examiner. Early next week, I plan to meet with Monique Lewis."

"Who is Monique Lewis?"

"She's the person who has been charged in connection with your son's accident."

"Why would you bother to meet with that woman? She was drunk. What could she possibly tell you?"

"I'm not sure what she'll tell me, but it's important for me to gather as much information as possible. If you believe Jamie's death was a murder rather than an accident, I have to examine all angles. Monique Lewis may have been drunk and a bad driver, but it seems unlikely she had reason to murder Jamie. So, if she didn't murder your son, it means someone else did. With no other leads, Monique Lewis seems like an obvious choice to interview whether she was drunk or not. Even in her stupor, her observations about that night have merit. When I take on a case, I consider every aspect until it's resolved, for better or worse"

Mrs. McIntyre sat back in her chair, her shoulders slumped, and she sighed. By the tone of her voice, I could tell she was unhappy about my decision to meet with Monique Lewis. However, by the reaction of her body, I could tell she was resigned to it.

"Shall we meet at the same time next week?"

"Yes, Mr. Prescott, that will be fine. Do you need anything else from me before then?"

"Yes, Mrs. McIntyre, there is one more thing. I would like to take a look at Jamie's bank accounts if that's possible."

"Yes, as far as I'm concerned, but I am not sure how you gain access to them."

"I believe you are the trustee of Jamie's estate. As such, you can write me a letter of authorization that will grant me access."

"What does the letter need to say, Mr. Prescott?"

On a page in my notepad, I drafted a few sentences for Mrs. McIntyre, tore out the page, and handed it to her. She asked me to enjoy another cup of coffee and cookies while she left the kitchen. In about fifteen minutes, she returned with a business-size white envelope, which she handed to me.

"In there, Mr. Prescott, you will find three copies of a letter of authorization, as you requested. I'm not sure where Jamie banked, but I assume he kept the account we established for him as a boy. In the envelope, you will also find a business card for Mr. Walter Thompson of that bank. We are good friends. I'm sure he will help you. Until next week, then."

Before I left, Mrs. McIntyre didn't package any cookies for me. I sensed that she may have been put off by some of the information, especially my intention to meet with Monique Lewis and the fact I still hadn't discovered the source of the clothes and shoes. As much as liked to make Mrs. McIntyre and, for that matter, all my clients happy, sometimes I disappointed them. The facts led wherever they led. Sometimes the pathway took me to an unfortunate end. During our next meeting, I would try to convey this notion to Mrs. McIntyre. I didn't want to upset her, but I didn't want to lead her on a wild goose chase either. Overall, I was pleased with the results of my investigation. In time, I just hoped she would be too.

20

File No. 16-12-07MCI

On my way back to the office, I stopped by Jamie's condominium. Joe Lawrence greeted me as I walked through the front door.

"Hi, Mr. Prescott. I was just gettin' ready to call ya. We finally got that computer fixed. My supervisor told me a little while ago that report you're lookin' for will be here by the end of the week, so ya don't have to be stoppin' by all the time. I can mail it to ya."

"Joe, thank you for the offer, but I would prefer to pick it up if you don't mind. Besides, I like to visit with you."

"Thank ya, Mr. Prescott, and no, sir, I don't mind ya stoppin' by one bit. I'm always happy to see ya. As ya can tell, not much happens around here day after day. I like watchin' ya do what ya do. Makes me feel like I'm part of somethin' important, especially when it's about Mr. McIntyre. He was such as nice man."

"Would it be all right if I went down to the garage again? There's something I want to check."

"Sure, no problem, Mr. Prescott. I'll write down the code for ya. You know the way"

I lifted the back of the cover on the Corvette to check the license plate. It matched the information Gwennie

Bedford gave me. Just to be sure, I lifted the front cover on the Corvette to make sure the front plate matched the back plate. They matched. I'm not sure what else I expected to find, but I knew for certain that no one had played fast and loose with Jamie McIntyre's plates on the Corvette.

Once I was back in my office, it was time to sit still and review my Jamie McIntyre file. I started with the toxicology report. Dr. Ortega had not misled me. Jamie McIntyre's blood alcohol level was low. To me, it suggested he enjoyed wine with his last meal. For his sake, I hope his last meal was a good one. Even men who have been condemned to death get to choose their last meal. The toxicology report revealed no use of illicit drugs, such as heroin, cocaine, methamphetamine, or marijuana. It also revealed no use of prescription or over-the-counter drugs. Jamie McIntyre's body was clean.

I turned to the coroner's report, which included all the information from the autopsy, toxicology and accident investigatory reports, and more. Coroners' reports are not to be read just before you go to bed. They are graphic in a clinical straightforward way—no adjectives or adverbs. The external examination record of Jamie McIntyre's body begins as, "The body is identified by toe tags and is that of an unembalmed refrigerated adult male, who appears about the reported age of twenty-seven years." The report didn't get better from there.

Next came the internal examination record. This could cause sleepless nights for those who are unaccustomed to these kinds of reports. Movies and television crime shows tend to glamorize the work of pathologists. It's a fine profession, but over my twenty-five-year career in the police department, I attended at least two dozen autopsies and know their work in no way resembles what appears on either large or small screens. My focus was on two items in the report. On page two, under the section labeled "Clothing," I saw printed: "shirt, pants, underpants, shoes and socks photographed, catalogued and bagged." Right after this disclosure, I saw in bold letters the cause of death as "evidence of external traumatic injuries and associated internal traumatic injuries." While I had hoped that the toxicology and coroner's reports would reveal new information, they just served to confirm what I already knew. Yet, I also knew something was amiss with respect to Jamie McIntyre's death. Some things still didn't add up.

I decided to focus, once again, on the autopsy report and, in particular, the body diagrams. They allowed me to see the extent of Jamie McIntyre's traumatic injuries. The report contained eight diagrams. I looked at five, which included front and back, head and neck, extended neck, left and right side, and cerebral. While I am no doctor, based on my experience, I know what to look for when I review body diagrams, especially those diagrams for victims who have been hit by vehicles.

For the most part, Jamie McIntyre's body diagrams were as I expected, with one exception. Three of the diagrams showed a significant blow to the head. The injury went much deeper than I would expect from an automobile unless it had an undercarriage protrusion. For the life of me, I couldn't think of anything other than a loose and fallen exhaust pipe that could have caused that kind of indentation in a skull. Based on my experience, exhaust pipes fall backwards not forwards, in which case it would have dragged over Jamie McIntyre's body rather than impale his body or his skull. At that moment, I realized it was important for me to meet soon with the driver, Monique Lewis, as well as examine the undercarriage of her car. She was at the top of my list of people to call later today, along with Jamie McIntyre's bank manager.

Before I made any calls, I turned to the condominium garage entry report. I discovered a stack of pages with hundreds of entries and departures. Of course, many of these vehicles were the same. They came and went in the same way I came and went from my apartment garage. What I had to do now was identify the multiple entries and narrow the list to one that showed vehicles only rather than entries and departures. These kinds of tasks were the ones I hated. They were tedious. Unlike the police department that has many resources at its disposal, when you work alone, you have no additional resources and get to do all the chores. This job had to be done, and I had to do it.

In order to streamline the vehicle plate sort process, I focused on the last three numbers or letters of each plate. In between multiple cups of coffee, I tried to narrow the list of vehicles, but the list was too long. It didn't take me long to realize that in order to identify all these vehicles, I would have to prevail, once again, on my friendship with Gwennie Bedford at the Department of Motor Vehicles. Hers would be a tough and laborious task if she would even consent to do it at all. On my way to Jamie McIntyre's office, I would drop by Gwennie's office and beg her to help me. I hoped she would do it out of our friendship, but I suspected she would expect me to take her to lunch. It would be well worth it.

Next on my list of things to do that morning was to call the bank where I hoped Jamie McIntyre continued to hold his accounts. I opened the envelope from Mrs. McIntyre and pulled out the business card she included. The name on the card was Walter Thompson. Underneath was his title. I was surprised to discover that Mr. Thompson was president of the bank. Obviously, Mrs. McIntyre moves in better circles than I do. My best bank contact was a manager, and she worked for a credit union. I picked up the telephone and called the number shown on the card. A woman answered.

"Mr. Thompson's office, how may I help you?"

"My name is Willis Prescott. Mrs. Lorna McIntyre gave me Mr. Thompson's business card and a letter of introduction."

"Yes, Mr. Prescott, Mrs. McIntyre called and informed Mr. Thompson that you would call. He's available to meet with you tomorrow morning at ten o'clock, Is that appointment convenient for you?"

"Yes, thank you."

"Good, I will let Mr. Thompson know. We will see you tomorrow at ten. Goodbye, Mr. Prescott."

Second last on my list of things to do that morning was an invoice for Mrs. McIntyre. I was surprised by the number of hours I had spent on the case so far. Her retainer covered them to a point, but it was now time to bill her for the shortfall. Even though the last time we met, our discussion had not gone as well as I had hoped, I was confident that she would reimburse me for my time and expenses to date. I was also confident she would continue to retain me through to the end of this investigation, whenever that might be. At that point, I was as less certain of the outcome of this case than I had been at its start. Nonetheless, I felt a breakthrough would occur soon and it would lead to a resolution. Whether Mrs. McIntyre would be satisfied with the resolution was another question to which I still had no answer.

I typed up Mrs. McIntyre's invoice and stapled it to my standard cover letter. After I folded them and placed it in a white business envelope, I affixed a first-class stamp. On my way to meet Mr. John MacKay, I would drop it in the mailbox outside my office. My thoughts turned to Mike White, who referred Mrs. McIntyre to me. We had not spoken since we last met. Until I had more information about this case, I decided against another face-to-face with him over drinks in our favorite bar. The next time we got together, I wanted to put substantive information in front of him to prove mine had not been a wild goose chase. With perseverance, I expected my case would be so solid that Mike would apologize and offer to pay for my drinks.

Next, I picked up the telephone to call the driver of the vehicle who had hit Jamie McIntyre. At first, I planned to show up at Monique Lewis's door but decided against it. That approach was too confrontational. She might slam the door in my face. If I wanted to obtain information from her, I needed to adopt an approach that was sensitive and empathetic to her predicament. Monique Lewis faced criminal charges that, if she lost, could put her behind bars and cause financial ruin.

On the third ring, a woman answered.

"Monique Lewis? My name is Willis Prescott. I am a private investigator and may be able to help you."

"Pardon?"

"Is this Monique Lewis?"

Her voice was hesitant. "Who did you say you were?"

"Ms. Lewis, my name is Willis Prescott. I am a private investigator."

"What do you want?"

"I believe I can help you with your case if you'll agree to meet with me."

"What kind of scam is this?"

"Please, Ms. Lewis, this is no scam. I know your case, and I believe I can help."

"Did my attorney ask you to call me?"

"No, Ms. Lewis. I have been retained by another party." It was now time for me to lay my cards on the table. "I represent a party who believes that Jamie McIntyre was killed in another way, not an accident. This party does not believe that he died because of you."

"Mr. Prescott, I have no idea who you are or why you would want to help me."

"Ms. Lewis, I promise if you'll meet with me for just a few minutes, I can explain."

Monique Lewis let out a deep sigh. It sounded like it came from a dispirited and depressed woman. "Oh, all right. Why not? What more do I have to lose at this point? When did you want to meet?"

"Why don't I stop by your house tomorrow afternoon around one o'clock?"

"I guess that would be okay. If I change my mind, how do I reach you?"

I gave her my telephone number and hoped that she wouldn't change her mind before our meeting.

The last item on my list of things to do that morning was to do something bold. I picked up the telephone, called my local florist, and ordered a dozen red roses. When she asked me where I wanted them sent, I paused. Where did I want them sent? I didn't know the recipient's address. So I asked them to be sent to Sutter General Hospital's emergency room, with the card addressed to Miss Lilly Chin. I hoped the dozen roses would make it to her and make a good impression, or at least one good enough to improve my chances when I asked her for a date. Lilly Chin got under my skin. She made me feel like a kid who had just been presented with a new box of crayons.

On my way out the door, my interest in Jamie McIntyre's business started to grow. Although I didn't know, and still don't know, much about computer games and applications, I was curious about the people who had made his business so successful. The name of his business was enough to make anyone take notice—"Gaming: The System." The name is a clever play on words and, to me, fits the industry. After I buy a computer or cellular telephone, I am never sure if my purchase is right for me. I always come home feeling I've just paid too much for something that becomes obsolete the moment I leave the store. The experience is akin to a new car purchase. I have always felt dealerships gamed me too. The moment I drive a new car off the lot, it depreciates by hundreds of dollars. To what extent, if any, did Jamie McIntyre's business game his customers? In a couple of hours, I would find out.

21

Gaming: The System

O n my way to Gaming: The System, I met with my friend Gwennie Bedford. I was both surprised and happy when she promised to have results within 24 hours. In exchange and as expected, she made me promise to take her to lunch. When I walked out of her office at the Department of Motor Vehicles, I wanted to click my heels.

As I parked my car at Gaming: The System and looked around, I thought the employees must be creatures of habit. All the cars were parked in the same spots as they were when I scouted the lot several days ago. Either they were habitual or all employees had assigned places to park their cars. The red junker was still there and still covered in dust. It looked like it hadn't moved in weeks and wasn't likely to move in the future. Perhaps it was abandoned. When I was last here, I was uncertain if I should ask about the red car. Now, I was sure I would ask.

When I entered the lobby of the building, I expected to see a directory of businesses. Instead, a large foyer and receptionist greeted me. A sign on the receptionist's desk showed her name was Debbie Smith.

"May I help you, sir?"

"Yes, Ms. Smith, I'm here to meet with John MacKay. I have an appointment."

"Your name, sir?"

"Willis Prescott."

"Yes, Mr. Prescott, I'll let Mr. MacKay know you're here."

Ms. Smith didn't suggest I take a seat while I waited, but it didn't matter because I didn't have to wait.

"Mr. MacKay asks you to come to his office. It's located on the third floor. He will meet you as you exit the elevator. The elevators are behind me."

For some reason, I had expected Gaming: The System to occupy a portion or one floor of the building. Jamie McIntyre was more successful than I had thought. True to her word, John MacKay was there with his hand outstretched as I exited the elevator.

"Mr. Prescott, how nice to meet you. Mrs. McIntyre speaks highly of you, although I must confess I was surprised by her call. As far as we know, Jamie's death was an accident. I hope we can help with your investigation. Let's speak in my office. Please follow me."

His comments were as brief as his handshake. As he spoke, I wondered on which side of Jamie McIntyre's death John MacKay would fall. Would he continue to believe it was an accident or would he believe it was murder?

John MacKay's office was in a corner of the building. I expected no less from a vice president.

His desk was large and tidy. I sat across from him on one of two leather chairs.

"Mr. Prescott, may I offer you coffee or some other beverage?"

"Thank you, coffee would be nice. I take it black with two sugars."

John MacKay picked up his telephone and ordered two coffees from an anonymous voice at the other end of the telephone. While we waited for our coffees to arrive, I made small talk as a way to ingratiate myself and gain his trust.

"How long has Gaming occupied this building, Mr. MacKay?"

"Please call me John."

While John MacKay asked me to call him by his first name, I didn't reciprocate and ask him to call me Will; I decided to stick with Mr. Prescott as a way to maintain a professional relationship. However, I don't think John MacKay noticed or cared. He seemed happy to oblige me in any way he could.

"We've been here about eighteen months. Before, we rented space in an old house in the downtown area but outgrew it within a year. This building came on the market, and we jumped at the chance to buy it. It gave us room to expand. Not all floors are full, but if we continue our current rate of growth, we expect to fill them within the next two years."

"Congratulations. John, how has the loss of Jamie McIntyre affected your plans?"

I sensed no reaction or discomfort in John MacKay when I asked questions. He seemed confident and revealed that Jamie took time to recruit and hire the best in the business.

He said, "Needless to say, we miss Jamie each and every day. But, I am reminded Jamie foresaw a time when he would play a lesser role in the company. He told us he would pursue other business opportunities in the future but knew they depended on the success of Gaming. Meanwhile, he fostered an environment where employees could flourish. He encouraged us to bring others along in order to make our company grow in new and different ways. Not only was Jamie creative when it came to software development, but he had business acumen. He put in place safeguards to ensure we remained ahead of our competitors. We are grateful to him for his legacy to us. Did you know our company was voted one of the best to work for last year?"

"No, John, I didn't know that."

John's speech was a great testimony to Jamie McIntyre. I was impressed. I then asked him about what he meant by "safeguards."

Once again, his response was just as straightforward as his last one. "I mentioned Jamie recruited the brightest and best employees. In order to keep us, he set up a stock plan so each employee could gain some ownership in the company and share in its success. For example, I now own twelve percent of the company. Other employees own as little as one percent to almost as much as I do. It depends on the number of shares each employee is offered and whether the employee elects to purchase them. Some employees purchase all the shares they are offered, some employees purchase some of the shares they are offered and some employees decline to purchase any shares. Jamie owned the largest number of shares. His stake represented fifty-five percent of the company when he died."

"Who owns those shares now?"

"His mother is his beneficiary, but we are in discussions with her in order to purchase some or all of Jamie's shares from her."

Mrs. McIntyre's ownership stake in the company was new information to me, but it made sense. "John, do you believe Mrs. McIntyre will sell the shares to you?"

"Based on our discussions with her and her financial advisors, we believe she will sell some but not all shares soon and then sell the remainder at some time in the future."

While I had an overall sense of the company, I still had no idea what employees made or how they made it. My investigation didn't depend on whether I knew or not unless it appeared to be criminal. If so, my investigation would be different. Any criminal activity could have exposed Jamie to outside forces over which he no control, such as blackmail. However, based on my discussion with John, I believed the company was a legitimate one. If I had more time, I might have asked him to show me what the company makes and distributes.

"What can you tell me about Jamie McIntyre's personal life?"

John didn't flinch. "Mr. Prescott, that's a tough question for me to answer."

For someone who worked side by side with Jamie, I was surprised by his response.

"Although Jamie and I worked together for several years, he always kept his business life separate from his personal one. Jamie wasn't much for small talk. When he was here, he was all business. Don't get me wrong; he was a nice guy, but he didn't share much about himself. He would let us know if he planned a vacation, but he never revealed where or with whom he traveled. If he came back with a tan, we suspected he had been somewhere warm, but he could also have got his tan somewhere cold, like on ski slopes."

I decided it was the time for me to change the direction of our discussion. "John, I noticed three white Lexus SUVs parked outside in the lot. Do you know who drives those vehicles?"

"Yes, Mr. Prescott. I drive one and the other two vice presidents drive the others. They're company vehicles. Well, the company doesn't own them. We lease them."

"Has Jamie's car been returned to the lease company?"

"Why no. As far as I know, Mrs. McIntyre drives it, which reminds me we need to transfer the lease and insurance over to her name."

I was surprised John didn't know the real status of Jamie's SUV. For now, I decided to withhold the information about it for 24 hours until I had a chance to see the updated list of vehicles on the condominium garage entry and exit report. "John, just out of curiosity, who owns the old red Nissan parked on the lot. It seems out of place."

"Mr. Prescott, we have no idea who owns that eyesore. We have tried to find the owner, but there are no tags on the car. We believe someone abandoned it. Although we could have it towed, we want to give the owner a chance to pick it up. We've decided to let it stay for one more week. If no one collects it, we will report it as abandoned and we will have it towed away."

"Perhaps I could help you identify the owner. My contacts at Motor Vehicles could trace the vehicle identification number."

"We thought of that kind of trace too. Unfortunately, the driver placed a road map on the dashboard, which covers the number. If you have any other suggestions, we would be grateful."

"Have you called the automobile association and asked them to open the driver's door for you?"

"Yes and one of our employees offered to use a coat hanger and unlock the door. We were afraid that the owner, if and when he or she ever returns, might report us to the police, so we decided against it. The car doesn't cause any harm other than it looks awful and takes up a space."

After we finished our discussion and commiserated over the abandoned car, I asked John about the building's security system. "Do you have any cameras pointed toward the lot?"

"Mr. Prescott, we do now. Until a few days ago, our system cameras monitored the entrances to the building rather than the lot. Once we discovered that abandoned car, we decided it was time to enhance our system. We should have done it a long time ago as a way to protect employees who work late and have to walk from our office to their cars. The lot is well lit, but lights can't help us identify anyone who may threaten or hurt an employee."

As I nodded my head, John led me to Jamie's office.

"Mr. Prescott, do you have any more questions or is there anything I can help you find?"

"Maybe later, John, but right now, I just want to take a look around."

"No problem. Jamie's office is just as he left it. To the best of my knowledge, no one has entered it."

Jamie McIntyre's office was just as neat and tidy as his condominium. Everything seemed to be in its place. Except for two flat screen monitors, a keyboard, a calendar, and, what I took for, in and out baskets, his desktop was clean. I sat in his chair. It was leather and comfortable, unlike my desk chair which, to this day, is vinyl and uncomfortable by comparison. I pulled out the center desk drawer and saw a collection of pens and pencils. Otherwise, it was empty. Each of the three drawers on either side of the desk contained miscellaneous office supplies that you would expect to find in anyone's desk. While still seated in Jamie's chair, I swiveled away from the desk to face the credenza. It matched the desk, but rather than drawers, it had doors in the center. I pulled on the knobs and they opened. Inside were an electric coffee pot, four coffee mugs, and a leather briefcase.

I hoped the briefcase contained Jamie's laptop computer. As I pulled on it, the briefcase was lighter than I expected. I placed it on top of the credenza and unzipped the top. Inside were some pens and pencils (each placed in the designated slots), a blank lined notepad, and some business cards—but no laptop. If it wasn't in his office or in his apartment, I assumed I would find Jamie's laptop when I found his SUV. But, where was his SUV? I was reluctant to go to Mike for police help until I had more information about this case to share with him. A police search for the SUV could wait for a few more days.

I returned to John's office and asked if he knew where I could find Jamie's laptop. "He carried it in his leather brief-case. Wasn't it there?"

"The briefcase was there, but the laptop wasn't inside and I couldn't find it anywhere in his office."

"Perhaps Jamie took it home, although I can't imagine he wouldn't have put it in his briefcase. Jamie took his laptop everywhere and, as far as I know, always placed it in his leather briefcase."

"John, I've checked his condo and it's not there either. My hope is that it's in his SUV."

"Mr. Prescott, I hope so too and I hope we find it. Jamie's laptop may have valuable development and propri-etary information stored on it. We need to find it and find it fast. It never occurred to me that it wasn't in his home or mother's possession. Now I'm worried and as anxious to find it as you are."

"Do you have any way to retrieve messages that Jamie may have sent and received on his laptop?"

"It depends. If Jamie sent them through the company's server, there's a good chance. For example, if he used his desktop computer, we can gain access. But, if he went through his personal or another router, then we have no way to access them other than through his laptop or maybe his cellular telephone."

Jamie's cell phone was something new to me and now something else I had to find. "Would it be possible for you to get me copies of Jamie's email exchanges for the three-month period before his death?"

"Whew, Mr. Prescott, your request is a big one. We have to consider corporate confidentiality and company policies, as well as our product security. But, I guess as long as we can remove any company data and information before we give them to you, it should be okay. Do you mind if I check with our corporate counsel first?"

"Not at all, but please emphasize to him the importance of those emails to my investigation."

"Why don't I call her now?"

My bias was revealed. Gaming: The System's counsel was female not male, as I had assumed. John got me another cup of coffee while I waited for him to call the company's corporate counsel. I heard him dial and ask for her by name. Then, I heard him leave a message, which also let me know I wouldn't leave with copies of the emails that afternoon.

"I'm sorry, Mr. Prescott, but Ms. Taylor is not in her office. Just as soon as I hear back from her, I will let you know one way or the other. If she gives approval, I will print, review, edit, and compile the emails for you. You can expect them to be available this time tomorrow. Good luck with your investigation wherever it leads. I hope you will let us know how it turns out."

I promised to let John know. We shook hands, and I headed to the elevator.

I left Gaming: The System with a good impression of John MacKay. He seemed like a decent guy. I hoped he could come through with the emails. Without Jamie McIntyre's laptop, I didn't know what else I could use to get a bead on his contact and activities in the months that led up to this death.

22

The Bank

Although my time at Gaming: The System had produced mixed results, it had still been a great day. As soon as I got home, I called Lilly Chin and asked her for a date. After she thanked me for the roses and we talked a little, she accepted. We agreed to spend the next Saturday together. I had promised to come up with a list of possible things to do and call back so we could pick what we both liked to do best. I was on cloud nine. That night, I slept like a baby.

I'm not sure what it is about bank vice presidents but they intimidate me. Perhaps it's because every time I meet with one, I am there to ask for money, whether it's a loan to buy a house, a loan to buy a car, or a loan to start my business. No matter how much information I give them or how much collateral I offer, they make me feel like I am a beggar and beneath them, which is odd because they are in the business of loans. The day I planned to visit Jamie's bank was no different. Even though I wasn't in search of a loan, my hand was out for information rather than money and from the president of a bank not a vice president. I shouldn't have felt inferior. After all, I had a letter of introduction to President Walter Thompson from Mrs. McIntyre. Just the same, I felt ill at ease even before I took my shower and shaved.

As the hot water beat down on my chest, I talked to myself, out loud too, as a way to build up my self-esteem and dispel my insecurities. As I did so, I also laughed out loud. I realized my uncertainties were silly. What's wrong with me? Willis Prescott never takes a back seat to anyone, much less a bank executive. While I shaved and brushed my teeth in front of the mirror, my confidence grew. My blue eyes danced under the overhead lights. Yes, when I met with Walter Thompson, I was going to meet with him as successful business owner Willis Prescott, who had questions to which I expected straight answers. The day called out for my navy blue pin- striped suit. It would make me look taller and smarter than anyone in that bank.

I pulled a paisley silk tie from the rack and tied a Windsor knot tight around the neck of my starched white French-cuffed shirt. Next, I brushed the shoulders, back, and front of my jacket. Once I was satisfied it was free from any lint, I put it on with a flourish in the same way I imagined Superman put on his cape. I studied myself from every angle in my three-way mirror and thought I looked good enough to grace the cover of Gentleman's Quarterly. It was time to take on Mr. Walter Thompson at the bank.

I decided against the drive-through at McDonald's for my breakfast. What if I spilled coffee on my tie or my shirt? The overall effect would be ruined. Instead, I took off my jacket and went inside.

The young man behind the counter was surprised to see me.

"You're much taller in person." I could see him try to recover from what he knew was a verbal stumble. He didn't do well. "I mean you look short inside of your car." Now, he just turned crimson out of embarrassment.

"It's okay. I don't often come in, so how would you know how tall I am?" I laughed to try and put him at ease.

It took me less than ten minutes to demolish an Egg McMuffin and hash browns, which I washed down with a cup of black coffee. On my way out the door, I threw the paper coffee cup, wrapper, and small box into the trash, while I placed my plastic tray on top of the bin. Not only was I full of food, I was full of confidence.

The bank looked like all other banks. It had fake columns in front of a fake marble façade, both of which I assumed were placed to make the bank look strong and formidable. From my perspective, a good balance sheet and a solid vault made a bank strong, rather than any exterior architectural features. The front door opened to a small vestibule. In turn, the vestibule opened to a row of teller cages on the left side and a row of office cubicles on the right. Across the back, I could see offices with doors and windows. I expected to find Mr. Thompson in one of them, but first, I had to stand in line and wait my turn. Three people were in front of me, although I found myself in front of a teller's window within a few seconds. He grinned as he greeted me.

"How may I help you, sir?"

"My name is Willis Prescott. I have an appointment to see Mr. Thompson."

"Yes, one moment please."

My life was full of these moments, which meant I had to wait. To me, they added up to lots of wasted time. The teller turned and walked toward a telephone. He picked up the receiver, spoke, put the receiver back on the cradle, and returned to me.

"Mr. Thompson's secretary will be down in a minute and will escort you to Mr. Thompson's office. Please take a seat." The teller pointed to chairs in front of the cubicles.

As I walked toward them, I wondered how much time I wasted every time I have been asked to take a seat. That day was different: just as I sat down, I heard a woman's voice speak my name.

"Mr. Prescott?"

"Yes."

"Please follow me." The woman behind the voice looked just as formidable as the front of the bank. She was built as solid as any bank vault too.

I did as she instructed and followed her in lock steps. The woman, whom I believed was Mr. Thompson's secretary, led me to an elevator that was tucked behind a cubicle. She said nothing to me. We went up to the second floor, and I followed her along a corridor to the back of the bank where I saw two large offices. She took me into one of the offices and introduced me to Mr. Thompson.

"Ah, yes, Prescott, you're here. How can we be of service?"

Mr. Thompson appeared like the epitome of every bank president I had ever seen on television or in the movies. He wore a gray suit, which matched his full head of gray hair. His low voice reeked of private schools and old money.

With the additional confidence brought by Mrs. McIntyre's letter, which was in my breast pocket, I adopted a tone of voice I hoped equaled that of Mr. Thompson. Of course, mine didn't have quite the polish, but it was as straightforward and firm.

"Like you, Mr. Thompson, I am a busy man and don't want to keep you longer than necessary. As Mrs. McIntyre may have explained, I represent her interests today. I wish to obtain copies of her son's bank statements for the last two years. If he had a safety deposit box, now is the time for us to examine its contents."

My approach seemed to work. Mr. Thompson didn't hesitate. In fact, he softened and referred to Mrs. McIntyre by her first name. "Yes, Lorna said you would need the statements and I have them ready for you, along with copies of any cancelled checks. As to the contents of the safety deposit box, in accordance with bank policy, I will need to see and make a copy of the letter from Lorna. Then, we will go to the vault and open the box together."

I nodded as he stood and handed me copies of the bank statements and checks, which I folded and placed in my jacket breast pocket. I stood too.

Unlike his secretary, Mr. Thompson spoke to me as we left his office and walked toward the elevator. "I don't know what to make of Lorna right now, Mr. Prescott. We've been friends for years. I knew her husband well and Jamie since he was a little boy. My wife and I were shocked when we learned of his death. Of course, we attended his funeral. But, we thought it was an accident. We had no idea that he may have died under suspicious circumstances. Until Lorna called me the other day, I had not spoken to her since the funeral. Of course, my wife sees her at bridge, but Lorna gave her no clue as to this investigation. I must say it came as a shock to my wife and to me."

I could tell Mr. Thompson's concern for Mrs. McIntyre was genuine.

"I hope Lorna has not embarked on a wild goose chase. Mr. Prescott, I confess that I checked into your background before you came in today. I believe I owed it to Lorna. You receive high marks for your abilities. Now that I've met you, I can tell you match your references. Please know I trust you to conduct your investigation and hope it leads to a conclusion that can put Lorna's mind at ease."

I wondered whom Mr. Thompson had contacted about me. Regardless, I was relieved that I passed muster and said so. "Thank you, Mr. Thompson. At this point, I am not sure what my investigation will uncover. Please be assured that, like you, I have Mrs. McIntyre's best interests at heart."

We entered the vault, and Mr. Thompson found a safety deposit box numbered 462. He pulled the long gray steel box from its compartment and set it on a table on a small cubicle. Then, he unlocked it with two different keys that were on a large ring of keys. Mr. Thompson lifted the lid on the box. Together, we looked inside. I don't know what Mr. Thompson expected to see, but I was surprised by what I didn't see. I expected to see documents. Instead, I saw computer disks and jump drives. Whatever documents Jamie McIntyre may have possessed, they were now on digitized devices. Although I had authority to take possession of these on behalf of Mrs. McIntyre, I remembered John MacKay's comments about proprietary information and company security.

"Well, Mr. Prescott, that's a new one on me. Based on my experience, most bank customers keep jewelry, valuable documents, cash, old coins, and precious objects in these boxes. I didn't expect to see a bunch of computer disks. Did you?"

"No, Mr. Thompson, I didn't. But, if Jamie took time to keep these here, they must have been important to him. As much as I would like to study them, because they may contain proprietary information about his company and its products, I believe it's inappropriate for me or anyone other than his company's corporate counsel to do so. If you don't mind, I believe we should get in touch with her and have her retrieve them in order to protect them."

"Mr. Prescott, I agree. Do you want to contact her or shall I?"

"If you know how to reach her, why don't you contact her; then I can work through her, if necessary."

Mr. Thompson closed the safety deposit box, locked it, and returned it to its slot in the wall. We exited the vault and walked toward the front doors of the bank. Mr. Thompson thanked me for my professionalism, which made me happy. As it turned out, I needn't have been concerned to meet with this banker.

"Mr. Prescott, from time to time, the bank needs someone with your qualifications to help us with, how shall I say it, sensitive matters that need to be handled with discretion. If I called you about such matters, do you think you could help us?"

"Yes, Mr. Thompson. Thank you for your expression of confidence in my abilities."

"You've earned it young man, you've earned it."

23

The Driver

On my way to my meet the driver of the car that hit Jamie McIntyre, I reflected on the case. Although Mike White thinks all cases should be approached like they are oranges, more and more I am convinced they should be approached like they are onions. While I followed Mike's approach when I was on the police department, now that I am on my own, I've found my approach adapts to the many variables that shape it. Often these variables overlap and have to be peeled away like the layers of an onion—they can't be segmented, like an orange, into neat and even sections.

Over time, I have discovered that sometimes an onion is well defined; sometimes it isn't. When I cut into a red Spanish onion, I can distinguish each ring, but each ring can be a different size and can have a different intensity. Even then, no two Spanish onions are alike. Some have more rings than others. When I cut into the bulb of a green onion, I can't distinguish each ring because there are too many and each is too fine to distinguish. Yet, just like the layers of a Spanish onion, the layers of a green onion bulb come together to form a recognizable entity with as much intensity. That's how I look at my cases. They're like onions, and no two onions are the same. I have to peel away each layer until I get to its base.

Jamie McIntyre's case was like a green onion—lots of layers, many of which were delicate. I wondered when I would get to its base. So far, all I had were clothes and shoes that didn't fit to suggest his death was anything but the result of a horrific accident. What I didn't have was more crucial to this case. I didn't have his SUV. I didn't have his laptop. I didn't have his cell phone. And, I didn't have anyone who I could point to as someone who would have wanted to end Jamie's life. Yet, their absence, along with the clothes and shoes, led me to believe that Jamie's death was not as the police department and coroner's office claimed.

As I pulled to the curb in front of Monique Lewis's home, I was impressed. Her home looked like a well-maintained Fair Oaks bungalow and, in this neighborhood, worth a fortune. If she lost her case, Monique Lewis could lose her home and more. The thought of such a loss had to prey on her mind. Her troubles were many and large. So, I was grateful that she had not called and we could still meet. She must have seen me pull up because as I came up the stairs to her front door, she opened it.

"Mr. Prescott?"

"Yes, Ms. Lewis?"

"Yes, Mr. Prescott, please come in."

The interior of Monique Lewis's home was as well maintained as the exterior. Monique Lewis appeared to be well maintained too. She is a handsome, well-dressed woman, whom I knew to be fifty-five from the police reports but her furrowed brow and facial wrinkles made her look sixty-five. I could tell she cares about appearances, all of which had made me wonder how she was found drunk behind the wheel of her car. It was difficult for me to reconcile the woman before me with the one who was characterized by the police. She directed me her living room.

"Please sit wherever you feel you will be most comfortable, Mr. Prescott. May I offer you a cup of coffee or tea?"

"Thank you, Ms. Lewis, a cup of coffee would be wonderful. I take it black with two sugars"

I watched Monique Lewis retreat to her kitchen. Despite the attractiveness of her appearance, I could tell by the tension in her face and the slump of her shoulders, this woman carried a heavy burden. Even if it turned out she was responsible for Jamie McIntyre's death, I felt sympathy for her. I've testified in enough cases against drunk drivers to know what was before her. The next several months, while she waited for her trial to begin, would be tough. Her trial would be tougher.

Monique Lewis returned with two cups of coffee. She placed mine on the small round table to the right of my chair. While I took my first sip, she asked, "Why are you here, Mr. Prescott?"

"Please call me Will."

She nodded and then said, "Please call me Monique."

Within a few minutes, it seemed to me that we developed a rapport on which I hoped I could earn her trust. In order to do so, I knew I had to reveal more about me and my relationship to this case than usual.

"Monique, first let me inform you that anything you tell me today will be between us. I promise I will not share it with anyone. As I mentioned on the telephone, I have been retained by someone to investigate the death of Jamie McIntyre. The person who retained me does not believe that Mr. McIntyre died as a result of the automobile accident for which you are now charged. So, in some ways, I guess you could say I am on your side. If I can get to the bottom of Mr. McIntyre's death, it may help your case. However, it's also important for you to know, my investigation may come up empty. If that's the case, you'll be no better off, but you'll be no worse off than you are today either."

Monique took a deep breath and sighed as she let it out.

"My attorney and have been over and over on this. I couldn't tell him more than already appears on the police report. So, I don't know what more I can tell you."

"I want you to take your time and recount the day, as best as you can remember it, from the time you woke up until the police arrested you. Don't worry if you forget details. If they come back to you as we speak, just let me know when they occurred and as you recall them. I'm not here to judge you. Instead, I'm here to flesh out the entire event on a minute-by-minute basis. I spent over twenty-five years on the police department before I started my own business, and if I do say so, I have a great track record when it comes to investigations."

"Well, Will, I woke up around eight o'clock. Since my husband died, I don't have to get up to make him breakfast, so I don't bother to set my alarm. Is the kind of detail you want?"

I nodded.

"I laid in bed for about fifteen minutes before I got up, put on my robe, and went to the kitchen to make myself a cup of coffee."

"Did you do anything else while you made the coffee?"

"Yes, I poured myself a glass of orange juice, which I drank with my pills."

"Pills?"

"Yes, Will, I take vitamins, as well as two prescription medications."

"Monique, what prescription medications do you take?"

"I take an antacid for gastric reflux and a mild sedative. Do you want to see the bottles?"

"Yes, but later. For now, please go on."

"Next, I ate a bowl of cereal. I like Frosted Mini-Wheats with skim milk. Oh, I forgot, before I went into the kitchen, I went out the front door to pick up my newspaper. It was at the bottom of the stairs. I read it as I drank my coffee and ate my cereal. Breakfast took about an hour."

"This is great, Monique. Yours is just the kind of detail I need to help me understand what happened."

So far, Monique was a good witness. As an investigator, I was pleased with her level of cooperation and the amount of detail she remembered and shared. We covered the next few hours in the same way: minute by minute. As she recounted her day, I discovered it was routine until just before noon. At that time, she told me about a telephone call.

"Maureen Masters called me. Her sister, Barbie, from Seattle, was in town and she wanted me to meet her. So Maureen didn't have to cook and we could visit, she decided that we should go out for dinner. I drove over to her house early so we could have a glass of wine and some snacks before we left for the restaurant."

"Monique, before you left to go to Maureen Masters's house, what did you do?"

"Well, after breakfast I tidied up the kitchen. I put the newspaper in the recycle bin, which is in the garage. Then, I made my bed. While I was still in my robe, I went out to the backyard to check on my plants, as well as pick any ripe tomatoes. I found several. I grow more than I can eat. Remind me to give you some before you leave. Are you sure this is what you want to hear from me, Will? My life is so mundane; I don't know how it can interest you."

"Yes, Monique, you're fine. Please continue."

"Will, I must say I find it easy to speak with you. You're the first person with whom I have conversed in over three months. I don't get to speak with anyone now except my lawyer, and if he has time for me, it costs two hundred and sixty-five dollars an hour. Needless to say, I don't call him often."

"What do you mean you don't speak with anyone?"

"Oh, some neighbors say hello, but they don't linger. Others try to pretend they don't know me. Even the women with whom I played bridge deserted me."

"What about your friend Maureen?"

"Will, after she heard about the accident and learned that I had been charged, she no longer calls."

"I'm shocked Monique. After all, you were on the road because of her. Surely, she has some compassion for your situation."

"You would have thought so, Will, but she believes I was responsible and should pay a price. Maybe, Will, she believes my behavior that night will reflect on her."

"Or, maybe, Monique, she feels some guilt."

Monique shrugged her shoulders. "Will, please excuse me for a minute or two. I suffer from asthma and I need to use my inhaler."

When Monique returned, she carried a glass plate. On it was a selection of cookies and pastries. She handed me a napkin and told me to help myself while she refreshed our coffees. I did. Her cookies were as good as Mrs. McIntyre's, maybe better. The pastries were sweet. One was lemon filled, and the other raspberry filled. Both sat on a shortbread crust. I was in heaven. While I sampled them, I thought it was an ironic fate that Mrs. McIntyre and Mrs. Lewis shared grief over the same tragedy. Both had to contend with it but in diametric ways.

"Now, Will, where did I leave off?"

"You were in the backyard."

"Oh yes, that's right, I was until I heard the telephone ring. I hurried into the house and answered. As you know, the call was from Maureen. We chatted for a few minutes and discussed where we wanted to dine. We decided on a new French restaurant near her house. She promised to make a reservation for the three of us at five o'clock, and I promised to be at her house by four o'clock."

"What happened after your call?"

"I made myself a salad and ate lunch while I watched some television."

"What did you watch, Monique?"

"The same thing I watch every Saturday: reruns of *Law and Order*. I love that show."

"I do too. Who is your favorite character?"

"Lenny Briscoe."

"Mine too."

"Even though I've seen most of the episodes before, I often forget how they end, so they're always new to me. That afternoon, I believe I watched three episodes until about three o'clock when it was time for me to get ready to go to Maureen's house.

"I chose my clothes from the closet and placed them on the bed. Then, I showered, wiped down the shower stall, dried myself off, put on my make-up, and dressed. I was ready by about three thirty. My car clock read three-forty when I backed out of my driveway. I arrived at Maureen's house a about fifteen minutes later."

Monique Lewis was matter-of-fact when she spoke. She didn't hold back. Even though her details seemed mundane to her, they gave me depth and perspective about her. I believed her. I also believe that I had started to earn her trust, which was vital. She needed to be comfortable with me otherwise she wouldn't be able or want to share the details of the rest of that tragic day. The day when she ran over Jamie McIntyre.

"When I arrived, Maureen offered me a glass of wine. They seemed to have already started to drink from their glasses of wine. While I prefer red wine to white wine, I noticed that they had white, so I decided to make it easy for Maureen and drink white wine too. Maureen had set out some brie cheese, almonds, red grapes, and crackers for us to snack on. While we sipped our wine and chatted, I had at least one piece of cheese on a cracker, plus a few almonds. About a twenty to five, Maureen suggested we leave to arrive on time for our reservation. We drank the rest of wine and took our glasses to the kitchen and placed them on the counter next to the sink. Maureen brought in the rest of the cheese, crackers, and almonds and put them away. Barbie ran to the restroom while Maureen and I headed out to her car. Barbie followed in a few minutes and sat in the back seat behind me. Maureen drove to the restaurant, which took about five minutes."

So far, I didn't understand how Monique became so intoxicated later that night. I was curious to know what happened in the restaurant. Did she get carried away and drink too much? If so, why would Maureen or Barbie let her drive home unless they were inebriated too?

"What happened at the restaurant, Monique? What did you eat and how much did you drink?"

"Will, once we were seated at our table, our waiter came to our table and presented a wine list to Maureen and menus to each of us. Maureen said she would wait to hear what each of us selected from the menu before she ordered the wine. As I recall, Barbie selected coquilles St- Jacques as her main dish and a Caesar salad as her starter. Maureen selected salmon almondine as her main dish and French onion soup as her starter. I chose the frog legs Provencal as my entree and, like Maureen, chose French onion soup as my starter. Because we chose seafood, Maureen decided on a bottle of white wine, although, once again, I would have preferred to drink a light red wine."

"Monique, your dinner orders have made me hungry for French food. Did any of you order cocktails?"

"No, we didn't. Another waiter brought a large basket of dinner rolls and asked each of us if we wanted one. We did. With tongs, he placed a dinner roll on each of our bread and butter plates. Then, he set three small shallow dishes of butter in front of them. He returned with a pitcher of water and filled our water glasses. Our main waiter followed him with the bottle of wine. He showed the label to Maureen and, with her approval, opened it. After Maureen sniffed the cork and tasted a small amount, he poured from the bottle into each of our glasses. After, he placed the wine bottle in an ice bucket.

"Our appetizers came soon after. We sipped our wine, ate, conversed, and laughed, like most women, or men, for that matter. The pace was slow and enjoyable. No one rushed us. The service was excellent. Our server waited until everyone finished their appetizers before he took away our plates. My best guess is that it took us at least thirty to forty minutes for us to finish our appetizers before our entrees were served. From time to time, a waiter would stop by to offer another dinner roll or replenish our wine glasses. Because I had to drive home later, I was mindful of the amount of wine I drank. My glass was replenished once between the first and second courses. Maureen ordered a second bottle of wine, but I had none of it. She and Barbie drank from that bottle. As far as I know, they finished it.

"Before our entrees were served, I started to cough and excused myself. I don't know what triggered my asthma. It may have something in the wine or the food. In any event, I used my inhaler while I was in the restroom. Within second, my cough subsided and I returned to the table. Our entrees arrived. We agreed the food was delicious. The waiter returned with dessert menus. Maureen and Barbie ordered chocolate souffles and cups of coffee. I opted to have just a coffee. While we waited for our desserts and coffees, I remembered to take my medication which I swallowed with water. By then, I had finished my wine with my entree. Maureen and Barbie replenished their glasses and continued to sip theirs."

"After Maureen paid the bill, we got up to leave. Because Maureen and Barbie had a lot more to drink than me, I asked her if she wanted me to drive her car."

"What did Maureen say?"

"It wasn't so much what she said as the look she gave me, which told me she was offended that I didn't believe she was sober enough to drive. I must admit, Maureen seemed okay and we made it back to her house without incident and without much conversation, which suggested to me I had offended her. Once we arrived at her house, Maureen asked if I wanted to come in for a nightcap or another cup of coffee. However, I didn't think she was serious, so I thanked her said my goodbyes to both her and Barbie. Then, I got in my car, started it, and pulled away."

"When you left Maureen and Barbie, how did you feel?"

"Will, that's what is so peculiar. Although I didn't drink much, I started to feel woozy. After I drove a couple of blocks, I turned the radio up loud and even shook my head a few times to try and make myself more alert. A sensation came over me. I seemed to have no control. When I wound down all the windows, I thought the fresh air would help. For a minute it did, but the sensation became stronger and stronger. Just about the time I realized I was in trouble, I hit and went over what I thought was one of those concrete barriers you find when you park your car. But-but, somehow I knew it couldn't be a barrier because I was on a roadway. I decided to back up, and I felt the thump again. I had no idea what I had run over."

"What did you do next, Monique?"

"I so was frightened. I couldn't think straight. It was like I was in a fog. I didn't know what to do. I have a vague memory that I should stop the car. I think I did, but even now, I'm not sure if I shut off the engine or just put the car in park. I sat for a minute, and it was like all my thoughts and my movements occurred in slow motion. I couldn't seem to function at a normal rate of speed. When I looked out though my windshield, I am sure I saw a large white animal. Although others think it was a hallucination, I'm certain I saw that large white animal. It had to be at least six feet tall. It looked like a rabbit, although it didn't hop. It ran from the side of the road and dove into bushes. I guess the thump of my car scared it off. Although I was frightened, I knew I had to get out of my car and check to see what I had run over. When I saw the body, I screamed and screamed and screamed. Those screams must have been heard by people in a nearby plaza because, all of sudden, I saw people surround me and my car. Then I heard sirens and more sirens. The people who came to check on me were replaced by paramedics and police. The rest of my night was a blur. I don't remember much more. As far as I know, I spent it in the back of a police car and an interrogation room."

"Monique, do you believe that tall white animal could have been a person?"

"I don't know what to believe any more. I guess it's possible, but who would be dressed from head to toe all in white? It wasn't Halloween. After I felt and heard the thump, I have no further recollection of how I got into this predicament, but I'm in it. Whatever I couldn't remember, the police have filled in. I'm in no position to dispute what they tell me."

"Monique, did the police administer a breathalyser test on you that night?"

"Yes, Will. Soon after the police arrived, they asked me to sit on the back seat of a cruiser. Once I was in the police car, I was asked to take a test."

"Did the police ever ask you if you were injured?"

"I don't recall."

"When they took you to the police station, did they ever call in someone to take a blood sample from you?"

"No, Will, I am sure of that. No one asked me for one, nor did anyone take a blood sample from me."

As Monique recounted the events of the accident, she became more distressed and overwhelmed by anguish, remorse, and guilt for her actions. Tears streamed down her cheeks. She tried to stifle her sobs with sips of coffee. At the same time, I could tell she didn't grasp the magnitude of what was before her. Despite her pain, I continued to question her. At no time did Monique resist my questions, no matter how difficult it was for her to answer them.

"If you don't mind, Monique, let's return to the accident. Did you ever see the victim through your windshield?"

She shook her head.

"Do you know if you hit the victim?"

"That's what is so strange, Will. Even though the police say I was impaired, I wasn't unconscious or asleep at the wheel. I never saw the victim other than on the road after I got of my car and saw that I ran over him."

"Monique, although you've said that you keep your calls to your attorney to a minimum because of the cost, have you spoken with your attorney about your defense?"

"I'm not sure what you mean. He's agreed to defend me. So far, that's it. That's all I know." "What I mean is, Monique, has your attorney reviewed the evidence against you and discussed his defense strategy?"

"No. You have asked me more questions than my attorney or the police for that matter. I'm so worried. If I am found guilty, I may go to jail, and at my age, they may as well give me the death penalty."

Monique looked like a beaten woman. NO wonder she looked ten years older than her age. I could tell she had no inner strength left to fight. She would need plenty when her case came up in court. Her success would depend on the skill and acumen of her lawyer. Based on what she told me about him, I was worried about her chances in front of a judge or a jury.

"Will, based on what I've told you, do you think I stand a chance in court or should I ask my attorney to negotiate a plea?"

"Monique, I am not a lawyer and not qualified to give you any legal advice. However, based on all that you have told me this afternoon, I do believe this case cries out for more investigation. I intend to pursue this case as far as I can, but my first obligation is to the client who retained me. Right now, I'm not sure if the outcome of my investigation will help or hurt you. You seem like a really nice lady, and my hope is I do help you as I try to get to the bottom of this case.

"For what it's worth, I recommend that you meet with your lawyer soon and ask about your case with respect to evidence and defense strategy. You should not be in the dark about these issues. Although he may have the best reputation in the world, his reputation won't win or lose the case for you. Facts matter, and it's important that he knows them all. To that end, you, not the police, are his best resource. Tell him everything you have told me today. Please also let him know that you and I met and be prepared for his reaction. Don't expect him to be happy about it."

As I spoke, Monique nodded her head. I carried on. "Monique, may I take a look at your car?"

Monique dropped her head, sighed, and told me she got rid of it.

"I do not want to be reminded of that horrible night. After the police towed it away and finished their examination, the nice young man from the tow truck company called and asked me what I wanted to do with it. I told Jason he could have it."

"Jason?"

"Yes, Jason Slack. That night, he was the only person on the scene who seemed to care about me. I will always remember his kindness. The car was a way to show my appreciation."

"Monique, that's a nice gift."

"Well, Will, I will no longer drive again, so why not give the car to Jason? He's in a position to make any repairs, and he told me it wouldn't bother him to drive it."

"Do you think Jason would let me look at the car and speak to me about the accident?"

"I don't know why he wouldn't. Do you want me to call him for you?"

"Yes, please, Monique. That would be great."

Monique got up and walked to her kitchen. I heard her riffle through some papers. A few second later, I saw her pick up the telephone receiver and place a call.

"May I speak with Jason? Oh, I didn't recognize your voice. It's Monique Lewis. How are you? Jason, there's a nice young man here with me now that is a private investigator and would like to see my old car and meet with you. Would it be all right for me to give him your telephone number?" A few seconds elapsed when Monique was quiet, so I assumed Jason was speaking at the other end of the call.

"Let me ask him. Will, Jason wondered if you could stop by his yard after you're finished here?"

"Yes, please tell Jason I would be happy to see him this afternoon."

"Jason, Mr. Prescott will be along to see you soon. I think we're just about finished here. Thank you, Jason. Take care. Goodbye, dear."

When Monique returned, she handed me Jason Slack's business card. "This has all Jason's information on it."

"Do you mind if I keep his card?"

"Not at all, Will, I have another."

"Monique, I want to thank you for your graciousness toward me today. I understand how difficult this had been for you and know what you face over the next several months. If my investigation helps your case, I will share the information not only with your attorney, but with the police as well. Otherwise, to the extent that I don't compromise my relationship with my client, I will keep it to myself. I don't want to cause you more grief."

"Thank you, Will. Please do stay in touch."

As I stood in the doorway to leave, we shook hands. Then, all of a sudden Monique hugged me and said, "Thank you for your kindness. It's so nice to speak with someone who cares and is not afraid of me."

I returned Monique's hug. Her comments about my kindness brought tears to my eyes. As a private investigator, I never thought of myself, nor to the best of my knowledge had anyone else thought of me, as someone who cares. I had three ex-wives who called me, among many other descriptions, "cold hearted."

On the drive from Monique's house to see Jason Slack, many thoughts ran through my mind. It was my practice to meet with one person per day. That way, it was easier for me to reflect on the discussion and compile notes, but that day, I had already met with two people and was about to meet a third. I knew, by day's end, my mind would be overloaded. My notes would have to wait until the following day.

My discussion with Monique left me with more than enough to assemble and reassemble against what I knew from police and autopsy reports plus other interviews. I now knew she was impaired not because of alcohol but because of a mixture of alcohol and prescription medicines. I'm not sure how much difference this would make to the police or to her case, but it might mean mitigation and make a difference to her sentence if she was convicted.

Beyond potential for mitigation, other aspects of Monique's experiences of that night disturbed me, not the least of which was the shabby treatment by her so-called friend Maureen and the subsequent treatment by her neighbors. Of course, I had to put sentiments aside in favor of facts. Monique offered new ones, if indeed they were facts. I hoped Jason Slack might offer more and, if possible, give me an outsider's perspective.

Because I represented Mrs. McIntyre, I should have held the person deemed responsible for her son's death in contempt. But after my afternoon with Monique Lewis, I couldn't. Just like the police investigation, I knew my investigation may prove her to be responsible too. Even so, I could still feel compassion for her. She was devastated by the events that befell her that night. Her life would never be the same. To me, she became more than just "the driver" of the car, she became a person who deserved help. To the extent I could, I would try to help her.

24

Jason Slack

Slack Tow, Car Parts, and Scrap Metal is located off Interstate 80 and about a thirty-minute drive from Monique Lewis's house. It looked no better or worse than any other scrap-metal yard. It's surrounded by an eight-foot high white metal fence topped with barbed wire. The yard is obscured at the front by large sheets of plywood, which cover the fence. I was surprised it was within the city limits. Like airports, most scrap yards are confined to areas where they can't be seen or heard. Of course, the construction of new neighborhoods on past vast tracts of vacant lands often brings them closer together which creates new sets of problems.

Jason waved at me as I drove through the gates. I pulled over and stopped the car. It didn't seem to matter where I parked. He put out his hand to shake mine as I closed the car door. His is a hand that most would describe as beefy, but unlike any piece of beef I ever encountered. His hand felt rough, calloused, and showed the effects of hard work in all kinds of weather.

Jason Slack is a big man. He stood straight in his blue jeans, I took him to be about six feet, five inches tall, with shoulders as broad as he is tall. By the way Jason filled out the black T-shirt he was wearing, I could tell he's muscular. At the time, I guessed Jason to be in his late twenties. It was difficult to detect the color of his hair because his black ball cap covered it and shaded his eyes. But, based on the color of his beard, I assume his hair is red. His eyes are blue like mine.

"How ya doin? Mrs. Lewis said you'd be comin' right over. What can I do ya for?"

I explained to Jason how I had been retained by a client, whose name was confidential, to investigate the accident. I also explained that both my client and I would keep his name confidential unless he gave me permission to share it. Jason nodded his head.

"It's about time. I been prayin' an' prayin' the police would take another look at that night. To ma mind, somethin' just ain't right. I'm glad you're on it. I don't care who hired you an' who uses my name." Jason had one hundred percent of my attention.

"Do you still have the car? And if so, can I take a look at it?"

"Sure, Mr. Prescott, it's a beaut. I couldn't believe it when Mrs. Lewis gave it to me. But you know what?" Jason didn't give me time to respond; he kept on. "I ain't plannin' on drivin' it. I'm keepin' it safe an' sound until Mrs. Lewis is ready to drive agin. She ain't guilty of no crime no matter what them there police say."

"I am curious, Jason, why do you think Mrs. Lewis isn't guilty?"

"Well, let's go on over an' take a look at the car. If you're a private investigator like you say you are, you'll be able to figure it out too."

Jason's strides were long as we made our way through a thicket of scrap cars until we came to a wooden garage. He raised the overhead door and revealed Mrs. Lewis's car.

"Now, take a look at that, Mr. Prescott. If you hit someone like they say Mrs. Lewis hit that guy, what would you expect to see?"

"Well, Jason, as a former police officer who covered many accidents, I guess I would expect to see damage to the front end, the car hood, and the windshield."

"Exactly, Mr. Prescott. Like you, I've been called to the scene of hundreds of accidents. I may be no detective, but I know what makes sense an' this don't make sense. What do you see here?" Once again, Jason gave me no time to answer. "Nothin', Mr. Prescott, nothin'. There ain't no such damage to that there automobile. An' I haven't laid a finger on it since I delivered it to the police yard an' picked it up after the police were through with it. What you see is what I saw the night of that accident."

Jason was right—the damage to the car was inconsistent with the accident Monique Lewis was supposed to have caused. But, I didn't want to express an opinion to Jason either way at that time. I wanted to hear more from him about the vehicle.

"Jason, can you tell me what the car is like underneath?"

"Sure, Mr. Prescott. When I cranked the front end up to winch it up onto the flatbed, I could see it was all just as it shudda been. All the parts were in the right places."

"Did you notice if the exhaust pipe or muffler were down?"

"I checked it all. Nothin' was down. Nadda. That car was as good as new. Now, I know Mrs. Lewis ran over him, so I saw a few bits of fabric, which coulda snagged from that man's clothes, but that's all."

I nodded. "Thanks, Jason."

Jason was a man who, based on the manner in which he spoke, may not have had much formal education, but he had plenty of on-the-job skills. Jason knew his stuff. I trusted what he had to say and wondered why the police hadn't asked him about what he saw. As a police officer, I valued all observations and all opinions, even ones which may not have matched mine. Based on his belief in Monique Lewis's innocence and his care of her car, I believed Jason Slack to be a kind and decent man.

"Jason, did you mention any of your observations to the police?"

"You bet I did, but they didn't listen. They just see me as the guy who comes to clean up when they're done doin' whatever they do. The funny thing is, as far as I know, I'm the only tow truck driver who actually sweeps up accident debris. The other guys just pick up the car and leave. Not me. I sweep up any broken glass and pick up anything that broke off the wrecks. I don't want any drivers who come after to mess up their cars with junk on the road. But I don't think the police on the scene ever even notice, which bugs me. I donate a lot of money toward the police Christmas party in order to keep my business name in front of 'em. You'd think they'd show some thanks. For what it's worth, though, Mr. Prescott, that night another guy seemed to be the one who directed all the investigation that night, not the police."

"What other guy?"

"That doctor guy from the medical examiner's office. First time, I ever saw one reach the scene before the police. Guess he happened to be in the plaza when all the commotion started. He didn't pay any attention to me either. I may only have a high school education an' I may only work with old cars an' scrap metal, but let me tell you, Mr. Prescott, I know cars, an' I know accidents. This one was the weirdest one I had ever seen in ten years of doin' this."

"Jason, do you mind if I take some photographs for my files?"

"Nah, Mr. Prescott, you go right ahead. Do whatever you want, but don't touch that car. I'm keepin' it safe for Mrs. Lewis 'cause I know one day she'll want to drive agin."

Jason walked with me back to my car so I could retrieve my camera. I still had more questions, and I knew I would get straight answers from him. In the meantime, I asked Jason to call me Will.

"Ah, Mr. Prescott, I'd like to, but my daddy told me to respect my elders. That meant callin' 'em by mister, missus, miss, sir, or ma'am. Guess I'm what other folks call 'old school.'"

"Well, okay, Jason, but when you call me mister, you make me feel old."

"Well, Mr. Prescott, you are older than me."

We both laughed.

"Jason, this may seem like a peculiar question, but did you happen to notice what the victim wore?"

Jason took a long deep breath while he thought about my questions and held it for what seemed to be minutes rather than seconds. Finally, he let it out.

"Well, I do sorta remember somethin' he wore that struck me as odd. The man had flared pants on, ya know, what they call bell-bottoms. Because he was dead, I knew I should be more respectful, but I remember I chuckled when I saw them and wondered where he got them things. I think they were brown. I also think he had on a striped shirt with long sleeves. But, something else was weird. His shoes weren't on his feet, but that's not the real weird part. The real weird part is they were side by side at his feet. If you've ever been at an accident scene, you know it's common for shoes to fly off the victim's feet when hit by a car. When they fly off, they can land anywhere but not side by side." As he told me about the clothes and shoes, Jason shook his head from side to side as if he was still in disbelief. "Yep, the position of the shoes was weird. The whole accident scene was just plain weird. For that matter, that whole night was weird. It's still weird. I hope you can make some sense of it 'cause I sure can't. And, if you do, I hope you'll let me know, and I hope you can help Mrs. Lewis. Nothin' would make me happier than to give her back her car."

While Jason stood off to the side, I took about twenty photographs of Monique Lewis's car from all directions and angles. As I shut off my camera, I turned toward Jason, shook his hand, and thanked him for his time, interest, and comments.

"No problem, Mr. Prescott. Anytime. I hope I helped you, an' I hope you can help Mrs. Lewis. She sure is a nice lady."

We walked in silence toward my car. Jason opened the door for me, which was no surprise. In the short time I spent with him, Jason struck me as a considerate and thoughtful man. That insightful man also helped my investigation to a great extent. With respect to the question about Jamie McIntyre's death by accident or murder, in my mind, I was close to a probable explanation. However, I knew a probable explanation wasn't enough. I needed a provable one. As to a provable explanation that would satisfy not only Mrs. McIntyre but the police, I still had more work to do. I hoped Mrs. McIntyre would continue to pay me to pursue it.

25

File No. 16-12-07MCI

The day had been a full one, and it wasn't over. On the way back to the office, I picked up a coffee at McDonald's drive-through window.

The woman in the window looked out at me and surprised me when she said, "You're out late. What no Big Mac? No fries? No Coke? No hash browns? No apple turnover? Are you sick?"

I just shook my head and replied, "Not tonight."

I was too tired to make small talk, too tired to laugh, and too tired to eat. By the time I got back to the office, my car clock read eight-forty, but to me, it felt like after midnight. I was exhausted both by the fullness of my day and the amount of information that swirled around in my brain. I counted on my cup of coffee to perk me up so I could sort, compile, and then transfer all of it onto my computer.

Before I could start the process, I had to respond to the red light that flashed on my telephone. It signaled I had messages to retrieve. I hit the button and discovered I had five new messages.

The first message was from Mrs. McIntyre. She called to confirm our next day's appointment and did not expect me to call her back unless I had a change in plans. I didn't, so

Mrs. McIntyre would be my first scheduled appointment of the day.

The second message was from John MacKay, who called to let me know he had copies of the emails from Jamie McIntyre's computer. This was good news. I was free to pick them up at his office anytime. He had placed the emails in an envelope, which would be available at the front desk. So, I scheduled myself to pick them up on the way to meet with Mrs. McIntyre.

The third message was from Gwennie Bedford. She had the list ready to show the owners' names and addresses of vehicles that entered Jamie's condominium garage. Gwennie said she would hand over the list to me when we met at Applebee's restaurant for the lunch the next day. Thanks to Gwennie, I now knew what I would do after I met with Mrs. McIntyre.

I didn't need the coffee to wake me up when I listened to the fourth message. It was from Lilly, who called to firm up our date on Saturday. Just as soon as I listened to the fifth and last message, I would call her back.

The fifth message was from Joe Lawrence, the front desk security officer at Jamie McIntyre's condominium. He called to let me know that the condominium guest list was now available. This excited me too but not in the same way as Lilly's call. For an instant, I thought I might be able to get to the bottom of the mystery sooner than later. However, my excitement faded when Joe explained that I would have to go to the company's head office to pick up the information. He explained that the company needed to see some sort of identification and some proof that I was authorized to receive the data. In his message, Joe provided me the company's address and the name of the person to whom I should speak. Her name was Sue Alsop. I planned to stop by and see Sue Alsop after my lunch with Gwennie. The next day meant another full schedule.

I erased all the messages but Lilly's, and placed the telephone receiver back on its cradle. I wanted to preserve her voice so I could listen to it over and over again. Before I returned Lilly's call, I finished my coffee, thought about the upcoming day's events, and created a schedule. In addition to my other appointments, I wanted to stop by the medical examiner's office on my way to pick up the envelope at Gaming: The System. After I met with Mrs. McIntyre, had lunch with Gwennie Bedford, and visited with Sue Alsop at the security company, I planned to shop at Harper and Hogan. After all my stops, what was left of my day would be devoted to what I called grunt work. It was an inevitable and important part of the job. I would have two lists to review, along with a pile of emails, all of which I would have to assess in relation to the information I received so far. It would take more than one cup of coffee to get through the next day.

That night, though, I had something more important to complete. This was not grunt work. This was special and not work. I picked up the receiver and placed a call to Lilly, who answered on the first ring.

"Hi, Lilly, it's great to hear your voice. I'm sorry it took me so long to return your call, but it's been one of those days. How are you?"

"Great, Will. I hope we're still on for Saturday."

"We sure are. I thought maybe we could play some miniature golf in the morning, have a light lunch, then catch a movie in the afternoon followed by dinner. How does that sound?"

"Miniature golf? Why not a real game of golf?"

"Really, Lilly, you play golf?"

"I sure do. How about eighteen holes? Then, after, if you still like me by the end of play, we can go to dinner. Why don't you bring a change of clothes with you so you can freshen up at my place before we go out again?"

My prayers had been answered. After three bad marriages and countless dates with women with whom I had little in common, I found a girl who was not only beautiful and bright but liked to play golf. How could I not like this woman after eighteen holes? I felt like I had just hit a hole in one, and we hadn't even hit the links.

"Will, if you have no preference, there's a course near my place that I enjoy. Would you like me to arrange a tee time?"

I ran through a mental checklist: beautiful, bright, plays golf, and likes to take charge. I was almost speechless but managed to eke out a "Perfect, Lilly." I wanted to say, "I love you" but knew it was premature. Just the same, I could feel myself fall for her in way that I'd never fallen for any woman before. I was almost sure I had heard the sounds of harps played by angels in the background. Of course, the music was just my imagination. This same imagination also saw me take my first swing at the first tee like I was Jack Nicklaus at the Masters. I hadn't even played my first hole much less my first round with Lilly and already I believed I had won the game. It felt great. I promised to be at her house by eight, with the hopes for a tee time at nine. She promised to confirm. We signed off.

Our golf date was in less than three days. I wanted to make a great impression on Lilly. It didn't give me much time to get into Harper and Hogan to buy new golf duds. I decided to drop in Harper and Hogan after I stopped by the security company. Perhaps I could kill two birds with one stone. With luck, I could pick out new clothes and, at the same time, meet Jamie McIntyre's friend Jeff Cousins.

When I thought about my need to meet with Jeff Cousins, I also thought about my need to meet with Dr. Miles Overstreet at the medical examiner's office, which was why I put his name first on the following day's schedule. In view of what I had seen on the autopsy report and learned about Monique Lewis's car, I had many questions to ask him. I had hoped he could help me reconcile the report to the car and provide greater clarity. It meant my day would start earlier than I expected, but it was important to learn more.

For now, though, it was time to focus on what I had discovered that day. I typed notes based on my discussions with each of the three people with whom I met earlier. As I did so, I thought about how I would frame my discussion with Mrs. McIntyre at our next meeting.

I decided Mrs. McIntyre would be unhappy I met with Monique Lewis. She wasn't happy when I had told her about my plan to meet the driver of the car, and I didn't believe she would be any happier if I told her about it. So, even though Monique Lewis was an integral part of my investigation, for our next meeting, I had decided to focus on Jason Slack's perspectives and let Mrs. McIntyre know I shared his concerns. More and more, I believed that Jamie's death was not the accident the police claimed it to be, but I didn't intend to share this belief with her unless she asked. It was premature. Too many questions with too few answers remained. Instead, I decided to let her know about my progress with respect to the data I received from the bank and the data I expected to receive from her son's company, the Department of Motor Vehicles, and the security company. I also needed to speak to her about Jamie's automobile and laptop. We needed to find them. Would she have any other ideas about where they could be found?

By eleven, I was beat. The coffee had long ceased to do its job. It was time for me to go home and get some sleep. It would be tough. My mind was agitated. A maelstrom of unanswered questions chewed on my brain like fleas on a mangey mutt. If Jamie wasn't hit by a car, what caused his death? No one, even Monique Lewis, had any doubts Jamie McIntyre had been run over by Monique Lewis's car, not once but twice. But if Jamie McIntyre didn't die as a result of trauma caused by Monique Lewis's car, how did he die? Was his death due to another accident?

If so, why did the medical examiner attribute his death to injuries he sustained from Monique Lewis's car? If his death occurred elsewhere, how did it occur? How did his body get to where it was found? And if it wasn't an accident, was it a murder? If so, why was Jamie murdered? Who did it? Where did it occur? How did it all come together under the wheels of Monique Lewis's car? I had too many questions on my mind and no answers to any of them which made for a fitful sleep.

This wasn't the first time a case cost me a good night's sleep. I also knew it wouldn't be the last. Yet, despite all my uncertainties, I remained confident I could come up with a solution. This case, though, was no orange with ten uniform segments. This case was an onion. It meant I had to peel away more layers. My problem that night was I just didn't know how many more layers I had to peel.

26

Mrs. McIntyre et al.

Despite so many answered questions, I slept better than I anticipated. The alarm woke me up at seven. I showered, shaved, and dressed. On the outside, I looked great. On the inside, I was a mess despite a good night's sleep. That day, though, I hoped to gather enough information from each one of my calls to help me find answers.

After I picked up a coffee and Egg McMuffin at McDonald's to drink and eat in the car, my first stop was the medical examiner's office. I arrived at eight, just as the doors opened. Heather was already on the telephone. While I waited for her to complete her call, I studied the photographs on the wall again. Right away, I noticed that Dr. Overstreet's photograph was gone. I wondered if he had left. If so, where had he gone?

When I saw Heather hang up the phone, I turned toward her. Heather didn't miss a beat when she looked up and proclaimed, "Wow! Twice in one month. To what do we owe this pleasure?"

"I hoped to see Dr. Overstreet. Where's he gone?"

"What do you mean, 'where's he gone'?"

"Well, his picture is no longer on the wall. Did he leave?"

Heather chuckled and said, "No, he still works here. His new photo will be up soon. He shaved off his beard and wanted to update his look. But, sorry, Will, you've missed him again. Dr. Overstreet started his vacation on Monday. He won't be back for at least another week. Too bad you didn't call first. You could have saved yourself a trip."

"It's okay. I got to see you again and that's always a treat. Will you make me an appointment for me to see him as soon as possible?"

"Sure, I'll do my best for you, but Dr. Overstreet handles his own calendar, so we'll both have to wait until he returns. Leave me your card, and I'll let him know he needs to call you and make an appointment time just as soon as possible."

"Thanks a million, Heather. See ya soon."

As I pulled away from the ME's office, I hoped the rest of the day's calls bore more fruit than my first one. Within ten minutes, I arrived at Gaming: The System and parked my car. As I walked toward the front doors, I checked the lot and noticed the old red Nissan was gone. I wondered if John MacKay had it towed or if the owner retrieved it. I made a mental note to double check.

The receptionist remembered me as I walked in. "Ah, Mr. Prescott, Mr. MacKay has left an envelope for you. Will you be so kind as to sign and date this release for me?"

I pulled my pen from inside my jacket pocket and scribbled my signature on the form. She handed me the envelope, and as I was on my way out the door, I stopped mid stride and asked her if she knew about the old red car.

"Yes, Mr. Prescott, we noticed it was gone. Finally!"

"Do you know if Mr. MacKay had it towed?"

"Oh no, Mr. Prescott. The car just disappeared. When we left work last night, it was there. When I came in this morning, it was gone. I was surprised. Mr. MacKay was surprised too, and so was everyone else. Mr. MacKay asked me if I had seen it go. Nope. It must have left in the night. None of us saw it go. But it's a relief to see out of here. It was an eyesore."

I thanked her for the envelope and, while headed back to my own car, found myself curious about who owned the red wreck and who picked it up from the lot. But, Jamie McIntyre's case already presented more questions for which I had to find answers. I had no spare time or money to find answers about an old red Nissan. Any more thoughts about that beat up old car had to be set aside.

Mrs. McIntyre led me to the back of her house where we sat in our usual chairs. She served chocolate chip cookies and banana nut muffins to go with our coffee. As always, they were delicious. As we sipped our coffees, I relayed my week's worth of activities to Mrs. McIntyre. She nodded her head. To keep myself in her good graces, I focused on the information from Jason Slack, rather than the information from Monique Lewis. While Monique's information led me to Jason, I didn't want to upset Mrs. McIntyre with revelations from the driver of the car who the police claimed to have killed her son.

It was ironic to me that Mrs. McIntyre held Monique Lewis in contempt. If she didn't believe her son's death was an accident, why couldn't she see that Monique Lewis was an invaluable source of information? Maybe deep down she did believe it was an accident but had doubts, and to allay those doubts, she hired me. But Mrs. McIntyre's previous reactions to the sound of Monique Lewis's name told me I should avoid any further mention of her.

As I delivered my report and focused on Jason's Slack's observations, I noticed Mrs. McIntyre's back straightened until it almost arched. At the same time, her eyes widened. "I knew it. I just knew it. The police didn't fully investigate Jamie's death. Mr. Prescott, you've found more information in a few weeks than the police found in months. What's next?"

I was surprised by the forcefulness of her reaction and her responses in as much as Mrs. McIntyre was reserved and seldom showed her emotions. She was the epitome of decorum. She had reverted to Mr. Prescott rather than Will when she addressed me, which caused me to sit up straighter.

"Mrs. McIntyre, before I speak about what's next, I have more information to share with you and I need your help with one item. Do you have any more ideas about where I can find Jamie's Lexus?"

"When you didn't find it in the condominium garage, I assumed it was parked at his office?"

"No, Mrs. McIntyre, it isn't parked at his business. John MacKay doesn't know where it is either. He hoped you might have some ideas. We suspect Jamie's laptop is in the Lexus. It's important that we find both. Jamie's laptop may contain sensitive and confidential business development information, as well as clues about how he may have met his death. If the wrong people get their hands on the laptop, it could spell disaster for Jamie's company. And whoever has it may be the key to unlock this case."

Mrs. McIntyre shook her head from side to side, and her cheeks went from rosy to red. I could tell she was angry.

"Will, I am dumbfounded by this development about Jamie's car, and I have no idea where it might be. To me, this is just another example of the police department's ineptitude. And, what did you mean that you need my help?" She asked that question with such vigor that even she was surprised. "I'm sorry, Will. I didn't mean to lash out at you. How can I help?"

"Mrs. McIntyre, now that we know about the Lexus, you need to file a police report, or do you want me to do it for you?"

Mrs. McIntyre put her head in both hands. She seemed to massage her temples with her fingers. Then, just as soon as she started, she stopped, put her hands down on her lap, composed herself, and spoke. "Will, will you contact the police on my behalf? As I said before, you have made more progress in a few weeks than the police made in months. I don't want to talk to them anymore. Please know I appreciate all you have done and hope that you will continue the investigation."

It was my turn to nod my head. "Of course, Mrs. McIntyre. I'll contact the police." "Will, I received your invoice."

"Did it meet with your approval?"

"Yes, it was in order. I have a check for you today. Do you need more to cover your expenses and fees?"

Well, that was a first: a client who asked if I needed more. Right now, it was enough to know she valued my work. "No, Mrs. McIntyre, I'm okay. I will continue to invoice you."

Except for a few pleasantries about the weather, we said no more about the case while we finished our coffees. As I stood up to leave, Mrs. McIntyre handed me an envelope, which I assumed contained her check, and a plastic bag in which she had placed a couple of muffins and a half dozen cookies. "These are for you, Will." Her voice was soft and solemn, like one she might use in a library or a funeral home. Mrs. McIntyre took a while to stand before she accompanied me to the front door.

For the first time, I worried about Mrs. McIntyre's state of mind. I wondered if hers was a case of being careful of what you wished for. Would she learn things about her son's death that she didn't want to know or hear? It was more important than ever to resolve this case as fast as I could. I hoped that all the information I gathered that day, along with what I had already, would further my investigation. I also hoped that Mike White would help me find Jamie's Lexus. When I returned to my office, I planned to set up an appointment with him. At the same time, I wondered how he would react to the fact I was still on this case.

I hurried over to Applebee's for my lunch with Gwennie Bedford. She waved at me from a booth as I walked through the front door and asked, "How are you stranger?"

We exchanged kisses on the cheek. Gwennie is a real friend. Our friendship developed over the years when I was on the police force. She was our go-to person for vehicle data. Although Gwennie is cute and fun, she's not my type, despite her natural curly strawberry-blond hair. I don't know why she hasn't married. She's a catch.

"Gwennie, I couldn't be better."

"Still breaking lots of hearts."

"If only, Gwennie, if only."

About then, our server came up to take our orders. As usual, Gwennie ordered fish and chips with a side of cole-slaw. I asked her why she always ordered the same thing.

"Because I can't make fish and chips at home like they make them here."

I surprised myself and ordered a Caesar salad with chicken. It was Gwennie's turn to comment. "What's this? Are you into health food now, Will?"

We both laughed out loud at the thought.

Gwennie didn't hold back. "Will, I've seen the type of food you eat. How do you keep that trim figure of yours?"

"Oh, Gwennie, it's in my genes. I'm just one of those guys with a metabolism that keeps me slim no matter what I eat or drink. It drove my ex-wives crazy. They were always on diets, while I've never had to do a thing to stay in shape."

After we finished our meals and gossiped about all our mutual friends, Gwennie handed me an envelope. "Will, all the info you asked for is in there. If you need more, you know who to call, and let's not make it so long before our next visit."

Gwennie and I left Applebee's together, exchanged farewell kisses again, and walked away to our cars.

So far, I was on schedule. My watch said ten after two. In less than fifteen minutes, I was outside the security company to pick up the condominium visitor logs, as Joe Lawrence directed. The building was larger than I expected. When I entered, a large counter was in front of me. It had to be at least twenty-five feet wide and about four feet deep. Behind it was a large room in which more than thirty people sat at desks. They seemed hard at work, either on their computers or on their telephones. On the counter was a bell, and beside it was a small sign that read: "Ring Bell for Service." I did. Within seconds, a person jumped up and came over to me.

"Yes, sir, may I help you?"

"Yes, my name is Willis Prescott, and I'm here to see Sue Alsop."

Without comment, this individual turned away, picked up the phone on his desk, dialed a few numbers, spoke, turned back to me, and said, "She'll be right down." His comment told me the security company occupied more than one floor of this five-story building.

Sue Alsop walked through a white door at the end of the counter. She carried a large manilla envelope. "Hi, Mr. Prescott. Joe Lawrence told me about your investigation. To the extent we can, we are happy to help you. I have the data for the period you requested. I'm curious why you didn't ask for copies of the video surveillance. I would have thought they would be of more interest to you."

I was nonplussed and embarrassed. I should have known an expensive property like Jamie McIntyre's condominium would have the best security systems in place. I should have noticed and requested any surveillance video, but I had failed to look or ask.

"Ms. Alsop, I didn't know you had video surveillance. Would it be possible to get copies?"

"Sure. I thought you might like to have them, so I have already downloaded them to my computer. It'll just take a few minutes to transfer them to a USB flash drive or DVD disks. Do you have a computer that can read what I give you?"

I hoped I wasn't red-faced when I responded, "Yes, of course I do. My computer can read all formats."

I felt like a dope. She must have thought I was a luddite. Who could blame her? I just nodded my head when she asked, "Why don't you follow me up to my office, and I'll download them. It won't take a minute."

Sue Alsop ran up the stairs. If I took them two at a time, I couldn't catch her. She was a lithesome woman. She held the door for me as I reached the top and led me to her office. Unlike the barren office landscape downstairs, the office landscape upstairs was lush. Sue Alsop's office was as large as the other ones we had passed on our walk down the corridor to hers. It had a big desk, with a large chair behind and two upholstered chairs in front. Her desk chair looked like it was made of leather. She invited me to take a seat and said, "I'll have a device ready for you in a jiffy."

By the time it took me to sit and cross my legs, she stood up and handed me a flash drive.

"I hope this helps. All I need is for you to sign a release for it and the information in the envelope."

I signed and dated the form, handed it back to her, and put the device in my jacket pocket. "Thank you, Ms. Alsop. I can't tell you how much I appreciate your help."

We shook hands and I left. The whole transaction took less than fifteen minutes.

While I didn't get a chance to learn more about Sue Alsop, she had impressed me, and I thought that if the company was like her, it had to be a good one. Hers was a company I would like to represent one day; although based on my failure to ask about surveillance cameras, I had suspected she might not have an interest in my services. Once my investigation was complete, I promised myself to use it as a pretext to call her and arrange to meet. That way, I could share the results, express my appreciation, and expand on the types of services I might be able to offer her company. By then, perhaps, she would have forgotten my oversight.

Next on my list of calls for the day was Harper and Hogan. So far, I was ahead of my schedule, such as it was. When I left that morning, I had two appointments: my regular one with Mrs. McIntyre and my lunch with Gwennie. The other calls, before and after those two commitments, were to pick up information so they were planned but unscheduled. They were also necessary stops. My visit to Harper and Hogan was unscheduled but necessary. Unlike the others, I had a twofold purpose at Harper and Hogan. First, I wanted to meet with Jamie McIntyre's friend Jeff Cousins, and second, I wanted to shop for more new clothes.

The door buzzed as I entered Harper and Hogan. My sunglasses did little to block the assault from the rays of the afternoon sun as they bounced off the window glass. It took a few seconds for my eyes to focus once I was inside the store. As a result, I didn't see the man to my right. I was somewhat startled when I heard his voice.

"May I help you, sir?"

"Ah yes. Sorry I didn't see you as I walked in."

"My apologies, sir."

"My name is Willis Prescott. Alex Harper and I are former classmates. I was in a few weeks ago and bought a few things from Alex."

"Well, Mr. Harper is not here this afternoon. May I be of help to you?"

He didn't introduce himself. However, I assumed he was Jeff Cousins.

"Yes, I am looking for some new slacks and polo shirts that I could wear to play golf or at any smart casual event. What can you recommend?"

"Of course, Mr. Prescott. If you will follow me, please."

I was led to a far corner of the store that is demarcated by red-plaid wallpaper embellished with antique sports' equipment. I caught a glimpse of a wooden tennis racket, wicker creel, fly-fishing rod, and wooden-handled golf iron. The decorations are tasteful and masculine. Before me stood wooden shelves with a wide variety of polo shirts in just about every color of the rainbow and racks of slacks and shorts in about every color and pattern.

Whomever this fellow is, his dress looked immaculate. He wore a gray flannel double-breasted suit with double vents in the back over a green gingham shirt with a spread collar. His tie was a paisley pattern in colors that complemented the colors of his suit and shirt. He is a little taller than me and just as slim. His ginger hair matches the hair of his well-groomed beard.

"Do you have a color preference, sir?"

"Well, in my line of business, I tend to wear navy or gray flannel slacks on a daily basis. On weekends, I most often wear khakis or blue jeans. However, as I mentioned to Alex, I want to update my wardrobe. What do you suggest?"

"How do you feel about pastels, like pink?"

I shook my head. "I'm not ready to wear pink."

"Then, Mr. Prescott, how about royal blue and perhaps some checkered pants or shorts in a madras print?"

I hadn't heard anyone mention madras since I was in high school, but I was game to look at something different. "Okay. Why don't you pull a couple of outfits together that you believe will suit me."

"Fine, sir. Now, as to sizes, because of the breadth of your shoulders and your height, I expect that you take a size large and tall in polo shirts. Am I correct?"

I nodded.

"And, with respect to slacks and shorts, I expect that you have a thirty-four-inch waist. Am I correct?"

Again, I nodded. This guy knew his stuff. I wondered if he could guess by pant length. I didn't have to wonder for long.

"I expect that your slacks are hemmed at thirty-four inches. Correct?"

"You're three for three."

I stood by and watched him pull polo shirts off the shelves and set them on an empty counter. Then, I watched him slide hangers on the racks until he selected several pairs slacks and shorts, which I assume were to coordinate with the shirts. As he displayed the outfits on the counter, I could see that he had a good eye for color. And, by what he had selected, he also seemed to understand my tastes despite the limited information I gave him. I was impressed and told him so. As a result, he seemed to loosen up a little.

"Thank you, sir. Because of your relationship with Mr. Harper, I didn't want to overstep."

"No problem. You've got a great sense of style. Perhaps I should ask for you in the future. By the way, I don't think I caught your name?"

"Thank you, Mr. Prescott. I'm sorry. My name is Jeff Cousins. I didn't know what to make of you when you came in and introduced yourself."

"Why?"

"Well, Mr. Harper told me that you have been retained to investigate the death of my friend Jamie McIntyre. I was uneasy."

"You shouldn't be concerned unless you know something that the police and the rest of us don't know. My goal is to find out as much as I can about Jamie in the weeks prior to his death. Any information you could give me would be most welcome."

"I see. Well, this is difficult for me. I hadn't seen Jamie for about four or five months before his death."

"Really? I thought you were great friends."

"We were, but Jamie found someone else with whom he wanted to spend his time."

"You mean Lilly Chin?"

"Oh no, Mr. Prescott, I mean Matt Alvarado. I broke up with Jamie when he started to date him. I guess our relationship had run its course. Don't get me wrong, I loved Jamie, but I couldn't compete with Matt for his affections. So, Matt would be the better person with whom to speak about Jamie."

Well, well, well. My suspicions about Jamie were correct. I thought it was a myth, but in this case, it was true. A long time ago, a colleague told me that you can tell a man's sexual preference by the numbers and types of colognes he has in his medicine cabinet. Heterosexual men have one or two types of aftershaves, gay men have dozens of aftershaves, plus a wide variety of colognes. I have no idea how he had come up with this notion. I wondered how many gay men's medicine cabinets he had inspected, not to mention why and when. So, I was skeptical when he told me, but I tucked that tidbit away in my memory bank. I have no idea why I decided to retain it, but I'm glad I did. It helped me understand Jamie better. Of course, despite all his colognes and aftershave lotions, when Lilly told me Jamie always behaved liked a gentleman with her, I couldn't believe any heterosexual man could resist her. But, as soon as I saw his medicine cabinet, I guessed that Jamie was homosexual and I suspected all those condoms in Jamie's nightstand were for a lover of the same sex.

Just when I had thought I was ready to tie up all loose ends, out of the blue Jeff Cousins dangled another string for me to follow. I had to ask.

"How do I get a hold of Matt Alvarado?" "You can't, Mr. Prescott."

"What do you mean I can't?"

"Mr. Prescott, Matt is no longer here."

"What do you mean 'no longer here'? Did he move? Leave the country?"

"No, I mean Matt Alvarado is dead."

"What?"

"Yes, I guess he couldn't handle life without Jamie and committed suicide within a few days of his death."

Whoa. This news came out of nowhere.

"Yes, I heard that he took an overdose, but I'm not certain how he died, except that he's dead."

I shook my head, expressed my regret. "Do you know if Jamie was involved with anyone else besides Matt?"

"No, Mr. Prescott. I don't think so. Jamie didn't mention anyone the last time he came in the store. However, he was with Matt at the time, so, of course, he wouldn't mention another lover if he had one. In any event, that wasn't Jamie's style. To coin a phrase, he was a one man-man, and he was circumspect about his private life."

I just nodded my head while I tried to take in all that Jeff Cousins told me.

"Mr. Prescott, have you made a decision about any of the shirts, shorts, or slacks?" "Yes, I'll take them all. You've picked out a nice selection."

"Great. Perhaps you'll step into change room and put on the pants so I can pin the hems."

As I entered the change room, I thought about all the information that I had collected over the last few days. It was a lot. A more conscientious detective would set aside his weekend plans and focus on it rather than go on a golf date. While I prided myself on my dedication to duty, I wasn't stupid. I couldn't or wouldn't pass up the chance to go on my first real date with Lilly Chin. The thought was too much to ask no matter what it meant to my livelihood.

The legs of the pants were unfinished, but I thought they looked great. Jeff chose well. I wondered if they could be hemmed by the next day so I could wear them on my date with Lilly. If not, I could wear the shorts. While I wondered about the slacks, I thought about Jeff Cousins.

Jeff Cousins seemed like a nice guy, yet I couldn't read him with respect to his relationship with Jamie McIntyre. When he spoke about Jamie, Jeff sounded dispassionate. His facial expression didn't change. Like anyone who has been thrown over for someone else, I expected Jeff might show some anger, some disappointment, or some jealousy toward Jamie's new love interest. But he didn't show any emotion when I mentioned Jamie's name nor when he spoke about him. Because Jamie continued to frequent Harper and Hogan, I assumed Jeff and Jamie remained civil after their break up, even if they didn't remain friends.

Jeff had me step up on a low stool so he could pin the pant length. As he did so, I asked if it would be possible to have the pants ready by the next day.

"I don't see why not, Mr. Prescott. Our tailor is here now. Let me check with him." I continued to stand on the stool why Jeff headed through a door marked "Private." He returned in a few minutes and said, "Yes, our tailor can have your pants ready by tomorrow afternoon. You can pick them up any time after two."

After I changed back into my clothes and exited the change room, I headed to the counter where Jeff waited for me.

"Thank you, Mr. Prescott, for your business. I will also let Alex know you were in this afternoon."

Jeff's voice remained just as it had for the duration of my visit. It never changed even when he spoke about Jamie McIntyre, Matt Alvarado, or his boss, Alex Harper. While he was an enigma to me, I liked his choices and I also liked the evenness of his demeanor. Like Alex, Jeff Cousins was someone to whom I would return for help with my wardrobe. I trusted his choices.

After I paid my bill and shook Jeff's hand as I bid him farewell, I started to drive back to my office. Like everyone else that day, Jeff Cousins gave me a lot to consider. I had also picked up a lot of information that I had to review, all which meant I had a long night ahead of me. I would need plenty of coffee and lots to eat. Should I stop at Perky's or McDonald's?

27

File No. 16-12-07MCI

Because it could serve up food faster than Perky's, McDonald's was my dinner winner for that night. I ordered three large coffees, two Big Macs, two large fries, and, for good measure, three apple turnovers in case I needed a sugar rush source as the night wore on. With my fiesta of fast food favorites, I was set to manage hours of grunt work and hoped my efforts paid off.

My first order of business was to check my telephone messages. I had three. One was from someone who wanted to sell me an extended car warranty. A second was from someone who wanted to update my business information on an Internet site. The third was from someone who was special to me. Lilly had called, as she promised, to confirm Saturday's date, time, and location. Her call gave me a rush greater than any apple turnover. I planned to play it again and again throughout the night or whenever I needed an extra burst of energy.

Next, I opened the envelope from John MacKay. It contained copies of Jamie McIntyre's emails. I don't know what I expected to find, but after I went through all of them, none revealed much about Jamie's personal life. All of them were work related. I put them back in the envelope, taped it shut, crossed off my name, wrote John MacKay's name on the front, and set it aside. I would to drop it off at John's office when I returned to the city the following afternoon.

Now, it was time to open the envelope from Gwennie Bedford. I hoped her list of names, which she had associated with the vehicle license numbers from the condominium garage report, would bear more fruit than the emails. Gwennie's job had been a large one. She had gone through over three hundred pages of vehicle license numbers and matched them to names. Looking at the report, I realized the importance of my request. I owed Gwennie more than an Applebee's lunch for her effort. I put my feet upon the desk and leaned back in my desk chair as I started my page-by-page review.

After four pages, my eyes started to blur—too many lines, too many numbers, and too many names per page. I needed to adopt another approach if I wanted to get through this report in one night. I leaned forward and grabbed my twelve-inch wooden ruler. I put it under each vehicle number so I could see the name beside it. Although tedious, this approach worked better for me.

Jamie McIntyre's condominium garage was a busy one. His name came up often. Many other names that I didn't recognize also came up countless times. I assumed they, like Jamie, were condominium residents. After a while, those same names started to stick in my mind, so I was able to gloss over them as I went through line by line and page after page and, instead, began to look for names that were uncommon or names that I recognized as a result of my investigation. After more than forty pages, I found a name I knew: Jeff Cousins. Based on the date shown, he visited the garage seven weeks before Jamie died. I was curious to see if his name showed up again and, if so, when. Jeff told me that he hadn't seen Jamie for about four or five months before his death. Yet, the garage records showed otherwise, unless Jeff went to the garage and not to Jamie's condo, which didn't make sense. I flagged this entry with a yellow ink highlighter pen.

After another fifteen pages, I saw Matt Alvarado's name for the first time. The date showed he visited about six weeks before Jamie died. Was this his first visit to the condominium or was it his first visit in his car? Had he visited before but as a passenger in Jamie's car? I hoped that the security camera footage would answer these questions. As I did for Jeff Cousin's visit, I highlighted Matt Alvarado's visit but, this time, in orange ink.

It took me another two hours to go through the bulk of the report. In that time, I finished one Big Mac, a large box of fries, and an apple turnover. I had about a dozen pages left to read through my weary eyes. Jeff Cousin's name had not popped up again. I assumed Jeff forgot about his visit to the condo after his breakup with Jamie, even though he struck me as a man who, due to the nature of his profession, remembered details. When I picked up my slacks, I planned to ask him about this visit.

What surprised me most was that Mrs. McIntyre's name showed up twice. Because of her close relationship to Jamie, I thought she would have been a more frequent visitor.

Matt Alvarado's name, on the other hand, appeared more than a dozen times, which, given his relationship with Jamie, made sense. The report also revealed that Matt, like Jamie, drove a Lexus, but unlike Jamie, Matt's Lexus was black.

What pleased me most about this report was at no time did I see Lilly Chin's name. Of course, I still had about two dozen pages left to review. But, I believed if she went to the condo, she went with Jamie in his car. She didn't drive herself. I promised myself to pay extra attention to the video footage to see if I got a glimpse of her, not that it mattered. After all, if it hadn't been for Jamie's death, I wouldn't have heard about Lilly, nor would I have met her.

The rest of the report revealed no surprises. Many times, surnames I recognized, like White, Ortega, MacKay, Overstreet and even Prescott, popped up and piqued my interest. However, when I looked at the first names associated with those last names they weren't Mike White, Henry Ortega, John MacKay, Miles Overstreet, or Willis Prescott. Those surnames on the report were just coincidental last names.

I set the report aside. The clock on the wall read eight o'clock. It seemed later. My eyes needed a break and so did my body. I had stared at the report and sat in the same position for so long, my eyes were dry and my body was stiff. I stood and grabbed my other Big Mac. I ate it as I walked around my office. It felt good to stretch my legs. After I finished my hamburger, I took a few sips of coffee. Like the burger, it had grown cold but still tasted good. I hoped the coffee would give me a jolt. I needed to be wide awake to review the security surveillance data.

The flash drive fell out of the envelope. I placed into an open USB port on my computer. All of a sudden, a directory appeared on the screen. Sue Alsop had created files for each month, for which I was grateful. I clicked on the first file and images of automobiles started to pass by one at a time and at a rate of one every five seconds. These images were of cars that entered the garage only. I made a mental note to ask Sue Alsop if the company captured images of vehicles that exited the garage too.

The quality of the images amazed me. Each photo gave me a full frontal view of each vehicle. I could see each license plate, but even better, I could see the driver and any front seat passenger through the windshield. As I stared at my computer screen, I decided to focus on faces rather than vehicles, although I did want to flag any Lexus vehicles, particularly white and black ones.

At the twenty minute, thirteen second mark on the first file, I spotted a white Lexus and hit the pause icon on my computer screen. I could tell it was Jamie McIntyre behind the wheel, and he was alone.

I hit the start icon and restarted my watch. I didn't think it was possible, but this effort bored me more than the report review, yet I knew it was necessary. As I reached for my second apple turnover, I realized I needed more coffee and more food to get through the files on the flash drive. I hit the stop icon, stood up, grabbed by keys, walked out my office door, got in my car, and headed to McDonald's. On the way, I now wished I had picked Perky's for my first meal so I could order something different at McDonald's for my second meal of the night. I thought perhaps I should try something different and more nutritious, like a fish filet sandwich or some chicken nuggets.

When I came up to the drive-through window, the attendant recognized me as he slid open the window. "Oh, it's you. Just a second, I think we've bagged the wrong order."

"Why? What is it?"

"Except for the coffees, it's not the kind of stuff you order. It's a fish sandwich and some chicken nuggets."

"Yep, that's my order."

"Really? Are you sick or something? Sorry, I shouldn't have said that, but I've never seen you order this stuff."

"It's okay, kid. Tonight's a special night."

He just shrugged his shoulders as he took my card and ran it through the machine, then passed it back to me, along with my bag of stuff. "Are you sure you don't want a Big Mac, some fries, or maybe an apple turnover?"

Just as soon as I sat at my desk, I tore the bag open along the side seams so I could use it as a placemat. But, first things first, I sipped the first of my three cups of coffee. It does taste better when it's hot. Then, I restarted the flash drive, returned to the file, unwrapped the fish sandwich, and took my first bite. I was surprised by how good the fish and cheese tasted and thought maybe I could get into the good nutrition kick after all.

No sooner than I had finished my fish filet sandwich, I noticed a black Lexus on my computer screen. I paused the image so I could read the license plate and compare it to the plate number I had highlighted on the report. It was Matt Alvarado's vehicle. Now, I could get a good look at him.

Matt Alvarado, like Jamie McIntyre, was a handsome young man. I guessed he was about twenty-six or seven. He had dark hair and was well groomed. Because he was seated behind the wheel of his car, it was difficult for me to gauge his height, but it didn't matter. At least now I could recognize him as I continued to watch the footage. I also noticed he had broad shoulders and a trim torso. His physique reminded me of a professional tennis player. His image made me wonder what he did to stay in shape. I suspected his diet was different from mine. Maybe he ate fish filet sandwiches.

By eleven o'clock, I had watched five out of the six files. What they revealed was unremarkable. It took me awhile, but in addition to Mrs. McIntyre's visits, I recognized Jeff Cousins behind the wheel of his car, a late model Honda CR-V. What was with Jamie and his friends? They all drove sport utility vehicles. I made a mental note to test drive one. And, of course, I saw Jamie McIntyre's image countless times. But, at no time did I see Lilly Chin seated next to Jamie McIntyre in his Lexus, which pleased me.

While I played the surveillance images, I played the results of my investigation over and in my mind. Over the past several weeks, I had peeled away countless layers of what I called an onion. Yet, despite what the many layers I revealed, I had not reached this onion's basal disc. I knew I was close and I could feel it. But, in my business, close doesn't cut it. Clients, like Mrs. McIntyre, expect solutions. I needed to find a solution.

Days ago, I abandoned the notion Jamie's death was due to Monique Lewis's car, despite what the police department concluded. While Monique Lewis ran over Jamie, not once but twice, he was already dead when she came on the scene and ran over him. Tow truck driver Jason Slack confirmed my suspicions when we met. But, how did Jamie's body get onto the roadway? Did someone place his body there? If so, who? And, why was he on that roadway rather than somewhere else? If he didn't die there, where did he die? How did he die? Was his death an accident or was it deliberate? I needed to find answers to these questions and fast. Mrs. McIntyre wouldn't pay me forever, and I didn't have forever.

I opened the last file on the flash drive and hit play. More vehicle images came up. I studied each one as I sipped a warm cup of coffee and munched on a cold chicken nugget, which I dipped in barbeque sauce—not a bad combination, although I suspected chicken nuggets tasted better hot than cold. It was now close to midnight, and I was tired and almost out of steam. Coffee had ceased to work its usual magic on me. The images on my computer screen didn't rouse me either. Instead, they continued to bore me and make me drowsier and drowsier. Nonetheless, I persevered for what seemed like another thirty minutes.

All of a sudden, a car came into view that looked familiar and behind the wheel was a face that I recognized but, in that moment, couldn't and didn't want to believe it. I replayed it and froze the image. I wanted to read the license plate to cross reference it with the report in order to find out the owner of the car. When I looked at this image, I discovered this car had no front license plate. Yep, I knew it! This car was the red junker I saw parked and deserted in the lot at Gaming: The System. Wow! Why was it at the condominium? And look who was behind the wheel. I stared at the image and tried to make it all register. The individual was someone I recognized. That was the bad news. The good news was I was now wide awake. With mixed emotions, I hoped this driver would show up again on the surveillance video. I needed to be sure.

More and more images passed by on my computer screen. I focused on each driver's face. In a few more minutes, I saw what looked like the driver again, although, this time, in a different vehicle. In a nano second, it hit me like a two-ton truck. I now knew I could solve this case. I needed to speak with Mike White right now and tell him the news. I reached for the telephone, started to dial his number, and stopped. It was after midnight. Despite our friendship, Mike wouldn't appreciate a call from me at this hour no matter how important it was or how elated I felt. The next morning would have to do. I shut off my computer, stood up, walked to the door, turned off the lights, and headed home.

As I drove, I wanted to shout out loud: I did it! I did it! But I didn't. Other drivers might think I was drunk or crazy. Neither was a good look at this late hour. This case had many layers. Some times, I wasn't sure what I would uncover. But, at last, I uncovered the last layer. I did it. All was revealed. I discovered the one person who could have committed this crime and get away with it—almost. It now made perfect sense, and I could hardly wait to speak with Mike. I started to think about how to explain it and how to convince him.

28

Mike White

Although I didn't expect to sleep well, it took the sound of my alarm clock to wake me up at seven. I knew Mike would be up. So before I even had my first cup of coffee I called him. Just as soon as he answered the phone and without any pleasantries, I said, "I've got to see you right away."

I'm sure he sensed the urgency in my voice. He replied without fanfare, "What for?"

"Mike, I've figured out this Jamie McIntyre case."

"Yeah, right."

"No, I mean it, Mike. We've got to meet."

"I can't this morning, Will. I've got too much on. Meet me at noon. We'll have lunch."

"Okay. Where?"

"Where else? Our usual place."

"Okay. Don't be late."

"All right, already. I'll be there. This better be good; otherwise, you buy the beers and lunch."

"Done."

After I showered, shaved, dressed, and ate breakfast, I had four hours left to myself before I met with Mike. While I needed about thirty minutes to drive into the city and another fifteen minutes to pick up my pants at Harper and Hogan. I decided to use the time left to me at my office. There, I could put pen to paper and draft an outline of the Jamie McIntyre case before I left to meet Mike. I needed to present him with an organized and cogent summary if I hoped to convince him that Jamie died under different circumstances than both he and the police department determined in their report. Mine was a tough job, especially when I still had a few gaps in my case. I hoped my friendship with Mike would enough to help bridge them.

For the first time in a long time, I didn't stop at McDonald's that morning for coffee. Instead, I headed right to my office. Once seated at my chair, I pulled all the relevant documents from Mrs. McIntyre's binder, as well as my own files, and spread them out on my desk. I grabbed a pencil and a yellow legal pad and started to compile a list of new facts about the case in order to convince Mike. It took me about an hour. Then, I typed it up on my computer in a format that was comparable to a police report, saved, and printed it. Next, I made copies of the vehicle report and the flash drive so he would have additional documentation not only to augment his files, but to support my claim. By eleven o'clock, I believed I had enough to convince him to reopen his investigation and go after the real culprit in the death of Jamie McIntyre.

After I spent a few minutes with Jeff Cousins at Harper and Hogan and picked up my pants, I headed to Alf's Bar and Grill. Mike was already seated at a table. As I approached, he said, "I ordered us each a beer."

"Mike, aren't you still on duty?"

"Nope, I finished up this morning, so you now have my undivided attention for the rest of the afternoon. So, what's up?"

For the next thirty minutes, I didn't sip my beer and seldom drew a breath while I relayed to Mike all that I knew about Jamie McIntyre's case. He listened. He also took many sips of his beer and ordered another. When I was through, Mike didn't say a word. He just stared at me for a long time.

"So, Will, based on all that you have told me, if we find Jamie McIntyre's white Lexus and the driver, we will find the person who killed Jamie? And you want me to reopen the case?"

"Yes, Mike, I want you to reopen the case."

Mike's face was deadpan. I couldn't tell what he thought. He stared at me some more. "Well, Will, as a minimum, we do need to find the Lexus if, as you say, Mrs. McIntyre wants to report it as stolen." Mike reached in his pocket and pulled out his mobile phone, then dialed a number. "Will, read that Lexus plate number off your report to me."

Then, Mike repeated the tag number to whoever was at the other end of the line and then asked for a BOLO, which stood for be on the lookout. Mike also made a detain suspect request and asked that he be called as soon as the vehicle and suspect were found.

Except when he phoned in the report and ordered his lunch, Mike had said little to me. I couldn't tell what he thought about my report. He continued to stare and sip his beer. Even though I knew Mike almost as well as myself, I didn't want to speak to him out of fear he might tear me and my report apart. The last time we met, Mike made no secret of the fact he didn't approve of my involvement in this case even though he was the one who referred me to Mrs. McIntyre.

All of a sudden, Mike let out a stream of questions. "Why didn't you bring me into the loop after you met with Jason Slack? Why didn't you ask me to help you cross-reference the vehicle report? What did you promise Gwennie Bedford to do the job for you? When did you connect the dots? Why didn't you call me sooner?"

Mike fired off so many questions at once that I didn't have a chance to answer nor could I remember all of them. But, his many questions told me that I now had his attention. Mike White was on side. He knew my theory was plausible. We could work together again and bring this case to its proper conclusion. At last, I could sit back, take my first sip of beer, and eat my lunch.

"Will, you know what your report means? I will have to reopen the case? And, you know how we hate to reopen cases because of all the paperwork? The district attorney will have my ass in a sling. You know that, don't you?"

I just nodded my head. Years of experience had taught me it was better to remain silent when Mike decided to vent. It was his way of getting his head around an unwelcome but important development.

"Jesus, Will, why do you always have to be so damn diligent?"

I just shrugged my shoulders. Mike didn't expect an answer to that question any more than he expected answers to all his other ones.

"So, what now, Will? I guess we just wait until we find the Lexus and the driver."

We didn't have to wait too much longer. Mike's cell phone rang.

"White here. What have you got for me? Where did you say? No, really? And, the driver? He's right there? We'll be right over." Mike closed his phone. "Will, you better drive. I've had almost three beers. You've just had one."

"Where to, Kimosabe?"

"Just drive. I'll tell you where to go."

29

The Suspect

No one was surprised more than me when Mike asked me to drive to the courthouse and said, "Pull up beside that patrol car."

I did as Mike asked and rolled down my windows. Beside the patrol car stood an officer.

As soon as I stopped my car, Mike jumped out of the passenger seat. I heard him ask the officer, "How did you find the Lexus so fast?"

"I wish they were all this easy, Lieutenant. We had just finished up in traffic court and heard the BOLO over our radio. As we started to drive away, my partner said, 'Wouldn't it be funny if that white Lexus over there is the one they're after.' So, we checked the plate, and lo and behold, it was the one."

"Good work, Officer."

"You'll have to thank my partner, Lieutenant. He's the one who spotted the Lexus. You've got yourself a humdinger. Your suspect won't shut up."

Mike walked around to the passenger side of the patrol car. He sat in the front seat and turned around so he could face the other officer and the suspect, who sobbed and talked at the same time.

"I'm so sorry. I didn't mean to hit him so hard, but he wouldn't listen to reason. I loved him more than I loved any man. Why couldn't he just love me back?"

Like any good cop, Mike said "perhaps you should keep quiet until you speak with your attorney."

"I can't! I can't! I've had this on my conscience for far too long. It's too hard. I need to let it go."

"Okay, okay. It's your life. You are now under arrest for the theft of the Lexus and for the murder of Jamie McIntyre. The officer will read you your rights and take you to the detention center. I advise you to contact an attorney as soon as possible."

As Mike got out of the patrol car, he asked the officer for his name.

"Wilkins, sir."

"Thank you, Officer Wilkins. You and your partner did great work. It won't go unnoticed."

Then, Mike walked back to my car. On the way, he asked the other officer for his name.

"Thompson, sir."

"Thank you, Officer Thompson. As I said to Wilkins, your work will not go unnoticed. Please take the suspect to the detention center and be sure to follow all procedures. We don't want this one to get away on some technicality. I'll meet up with you later. While I'm here, I have to see the district attorney."

Mike signaled me to come with him. I pulled my car into an empty spot, rolled up my windows, got out, and locked my car. Mike turned to me.

"Let's go see the district attorney while we're here. I might as well face the music now rather than later. By the way, Will, you know you have ruined my Friday afternoon and most likely my entire weekend."

"Sorry, Mike, but I know you would rather see the right person charged and justice done than enjoy your weekend."

"Yeah, I guess, but I also would have liked to have been the person who solved this case the first time around. I'm sorry I doubted you when you took on the case."

"Well, you can take comfort in the fact that you are the one who recommended me."

30

The District Attorney's Office

M ike White brought District Attorney Edgar Pruitt up to speed on the developments in the Jamie McIntyre case. Edgar Pruitt was as shocked as Mike White. He thanked me for my work on the case and agreed that Monique Lewis should no longer be considered a suspect. He directed Mike to speak to Wendy Carver. She was the assistant district attorney who had been assigned to the Jamie McIntyre case.

We discovered that Ms. Carver was one of the younger ADAs on staff. She's a looker but I could tell she's all business. If this case wasn't so serious and if I wasn't so taken with Lilly Chin, I might have tried to make a move. Mike explained the developments in the case and the results of our discussion with District Attorney Pruitt. Ms. Carver nodded.

"So, Lieutenant White, how do you want to handle this?"

"Well, Ms. Carver, later today I will interrogate the suspect. But, based on the suspect's outbursts to me and to the officers on the scene, my interrogation should be a formality. I am confident that we have the right person. Right now, I need some direction with regard to Monique Lewis. I don't think it's fair for her to be kept in limbo."

"I agree. Do you want me to contact her?"

"If you have no objection, Ms. Carver, Will and I would like to tell her. And, with your permission, both Will and I would like to inform Mrs. McIntyre. After all, it was because of her that Will was brought on to this case."

"Okay. I'll prepare the paperwork to drop the charges against Monique Lewis. You can inform her that she will receive formal notice within a few days. I still have a problem with the fact she ran over Jamie McIntyre, but given all that you have told me about what happened to her that night, I think this is one I have to let go."

"Thank you, Ms. Carver. We'll let Ms. Lewis know."

We left Ms. Carver's office and walked down the hall toward the elevators.

"Will, I guess we should go back to Alf's so I can pick up my car."

"Yeah, Mike, and you can pay the bill."

"Gosh, we left in such a hurry, I forgot. I guess it's the least I can do for you." Mike slapped me on the back, then put his arm around me as we approached my car.

31

Monique Lewis

I pulled up in front of Monique Lewis's house a few minutes ahead of Mike. As soon as he arrived, I got out of my car, and together, we walked up to her front door. Mike pushed her doorbell. When Monique opened her door and saw the two of us before her, I could tell she was frightened, so I spoke first.

"Monique, Lieutenant White and I are here to share some good news. May we come in?"

"Of course, Will, Lieutenant White, please come in. What news? What is it?"

Monique directed us to her living room. We sat on either end of her sofa. Mike explained some of the developments in the case. To her delight, Mike explained to Monique that all charges against her would be dropped and that she would receive formal notification within a few days. For the first time, I saw Monique Lewis relax. All the tension left not only body but her face. The change in her facial expression was so rapid and dramatic, you might have been tempted to think she had been transformed by plastic surgery.

"Oh, Lieutenant White, I can't thank you enough for this news."

"All the thanks belong to Will. He's the one who solved this case. I wish I could share more information with you, but because the case is still in the works, I am unable to do so."

Now, I could tell that Monique wanted to hear more. The last few months had almost destroyed her. Now that she was off the hook, she needed to know why. I planned to tell her the full story as soon as possible. But, Mike and I needed to see Mrs. McIntyre before the press beat us to it. We stood to leave.

"Monique, why don't I stop by on Monday and fill you in on all the details? I bet you would like to know more about the big white rabbit you saw that night."

"You bet I would, Will. I can hardly wait. Come as soon as you can on Monday." Monique's excitement was palpable. "I'll have the coffee on, and I'll make you some of those tarts and cookies you like."

Mike and I thanked Monique. We headed out to see Mrs. McIntyre. As he opened his car door, Mike turned to me and asked, "How come you get coffee and cookies?"

"I guess I'm more handsome and have more charm than you do. As it turns out, I'm a better detective too." I wasn't sure if Mike snickered or scowled as he got into his car.

32

Mrs. McIntyre

We encountered Friday afternoon rush hour traffic as we made our way across the city toward the Fabulous Forties. It was five o'clock by the time we arrived. I didn't want to interrupt Mrs. McIntyre's dinner. However, given the developments in Jamie's case, I believed she would forgive us.

As Mike and I stood outside Mrs. McIntyre's front door, Mike remarked, "Wow, this is quite the place. I've never been in one of these houses. I guess I've never gotten called out here on a case."

This time, I rapped the door knocker. A couple of minutes went by, and we received no response. I wondered if Mrs. McIntyre was out. Just as I was about to rap again, the front door opened.

"Why Will, what brings you here? Did we have an appointment?"

"No, Mrs. McIntyre. There have been significant developments in your son's case. Lieutenant White and I wanted to share them with you as soon as possible and before the press gets their hands on this story."

Unlike Monique Lewis, who relaxed when we told about these new developments, I could see Mrs. McIntyre grow tense.

"Please come in."

Instead of the kitchen, Mrs. McIntyre led us to her living room.

"May I offer you gentlemen something? Perhaps coffee, tea, soda, or something stronger?"

"I would love a cup of coffee, Mrs. McIntyre."

"The usual, Will?"

"Yes, please."

"And you, Lieutenant White?

"No, thanks, Mrs. McIntyre. I'm good."

In about five minutes, Mrs. McIntyre returned with two cups of coffee: one for her and one for me. This time, Mike deferred to me to explain the developments in her son's case. I handed her a copy of the report that I gave Mike earlier in the day. Then I went through it line by line. As I went along, it was tough for me to gauge the extent of her reaction. Her brow furrowed, and her eyes grew wide. When I was through, I asked if she had any questions.

"Will, this is all so much to absorb. Do you mean to tell me that the assistant medical examiner killed Jamie?"

"Yes, this afternoon both Lieutenant White and I heard him confess to the crime just before the officers placed him under arrest."

"But, why? How?"

This was the part I dreaded to tell her about. I suspected that Mrs. McIntyre had no idea her son was a homosexual. No matter how much I tried to dance around the subject, she had to know the whole story, but I would try as much as possible to avoid sexual references with respect to Jamie.

"Mrs. McIntyre, it seems that Dr. Overstreet fell in love with your son. He became obsessed with him. When your son did not reciprocate, he became jealous of the relationship your son had with another person."

"Will, do you mean Lilly Chin?"

"No, Mrs. McIntyre, someone else."

Unless she asked, I had no plans to tell her then. If she pursued it, I would wait until later in the week after she had a chance to digest everything. However, I suspected Mrs. McIntyre wouldn't want to know, so I wouldn't have to tell her. Instead, I focused on the events of Jamie's death and told her, "In a fit of anger, Dr. Overstreet struck Jamie. He claims that he didn't mean to kill him, but he did. In his capacity as assistant medical examiner, Dr. Overstreet was in a position to cover up the crime. After he struck and killed Jamie, I'm sure his head injury meant a lot of blood. So, after Dr. Overstreet cleaned Jamie and the crime scene, he took off Jamie's bloody clothes and dressed him in other clothes, which probably came out of his own wardrobe. Then, he brought in the medical examiner's van to your son's condominium garage, loaded Jamie's body, and took it to the roadway where he staged an accident. He then parked the van in the lot at the nearby strip mall and waited in a coffee shop until someone ran over Jamie. When he heard the screams, Dr. Overstreet, like the others in the coffee shop, ran out to see what happened. Dr. Overstreet pretended to offer aid and comfort to Jamie, even though he knew he was dead. To the officers and paramedics who arrived next, he claimed to be on the way home from another call. Dr. Overstreet may have gotten away with his crime if you hadn't noticed that Jamie's clothes and shoes were all wrong."

This was a lot of information to unload on Mrs. McIntyre at one time. I tried to be sensitive and to pace the details as I shared them with her. I wanted to spare her from more hurt. She was a strong woman, but this, after all, was about the tragic death of her son—her only child. In order to give both her and me a break, I stopped and took a few sips of my cup of coffee.

"I know this is a lot to take in, Mrs. McIntyre. Do you have any questions for me now or would you like me to come back in a few days?"

"Will, why would Dr. Overstreet think my son would be interested in a relationship with him? It doesn't make any sense to me."

I had hoped she wouldn't ask this question because I knew the answer would upset her, so I stalled. I took sips of my coffee while I tried to come up with a plausible response to work around her son's homosexuality. Before I could come up with something, Mike laid bare what I hoped to avoid.

"Mrs. McIntyre, Dr. Overstreet was jealous of your son's relationship with Matt Alvarado. As you may know, Matt was so distraught when he learned of Jamie's death that he committed suicide."

Mrs. McIntyre turned white and grew cold. She stared at Mike White and, in a voice that I had never heard before, said, "I know nothing of the sort, Lieutenant White, and I resent your implications about my son. Please stop. You have no right to make those accusations, especially when you are the one who failed to find my son's real killer. I must ask you to leave my house at once. Get out!"

Mike's lower jaw dropped. His mouth hung open. I could tell Mike was at a loss, but he did as Mrs. McIntyre commanded. He got up and left. Mrs. McIntyre and I sat in silence for a long time. At last, she asked, "Will, is what Lieutenant White said true?"

I didn't want to say the words out loud because I knew they would hurt her even more. So, I just nodded my head.

Mrs. McIntyre slumped down in her seat. Her body caved in around her like a tent in a tornado. We sat in silence again. She broke the silence and, in a quiet voice, said, "Will, if you don't mind, I would like to be on my own now."

I nodded and, for the first time, showed myself out Mrs. McIntyre's front door. Although I didn't know it then, that night I saw Mrs. McIntyre for the last time. Even though I hadn't said the words out loud, I found out things about her son she didn't want to know or hear. What's worse, Mrs. McIntyre knew she had paid me to find them.

33

Lilly Chin

I returned to my office by eight o'clock. After I left Mrs. McIntyre, I stopped by Perky's for something to eat, but I wasn't hungry. I was depressed. Yet, I should have been happy and ready to celebrate. I solved Jamie McIntyre's murder. Monique Lewis was a free woman. But my client, Mrs. McIntyre was unhappy and that made me unhappy. In some ways, mine is a strange business. This time, when I gave the customer what she wanted to know, she received more than she wanted to hear.

The light on my telephone flashed. I had three messages. The first was from Walter Thompson, who wanted to see me next week about a couple of issues at the bank. He asked me to call him back on Monday. The next was from someone who wanted to offer me an extended warranty on my car. I didn't bother to write down that name and number. It delighted me to delete that message. The third message raised my spirits. It was from Lilly Chin.

"'Hi, Will. It's Lilly. Sorry, but I have to break our golf date for tomorrow. We're short staffed. I've been called into work.'"

I couldn't believe it. My heart sank. The times when I was so tired and wanted to fold, the prospect of this date with Lilly kept me buoyant.

Lilly went on to say, "I hope you're not too disappointed. Why don't you come to my place and I'll cook us dinner. That way we can spend a quiet night together. If your week has been anything like mine, you'll want to relax. Call me when you get this message."

My spirits lifted. I could feel myself grin. Lilly Chin was a gift.

I sat straight, threw my shoulders back, picked up the telephone receiver, and dialed Lilly's number. She answered on the second ring.

"Hello, stranger. You got my message. I hoped you would call before I went to bed for the night."

"I did get your message and it cheered me. Your idea for tomorrow night sounds great. What can I bring and what time do you want me at your house?"

"Wonderful, Will. If you have a wine preference, why don't you bring it. Otherwise, I just want to see your smile and enjoy your company. I should be home from work by four. Come any time after. It's been a tough week."

I didn't want to disturb her sleep with news about Jamie. It could keep until our date.

"It's been tough week for me too. I'll tell you about it over a glass of wine or two tomorrow night. Until then, Lilly, I hope you have pleasant dreams."

"I hope you do too, Will."

Saturday night and Sunday morning were all that I dreamed they could be. I was infatuated with Lilly Chin, and I believe she felt the same away about me. Not only was she beautiful, but she was a fabulous cook. I helped her make the salad as we sipped wine. After we ate our salads, Lilly served an anti-pasta plate. It had all my favorites: roasted red peppers, pickled onions, salami, parmesan cheese, and crusty Italian bread. If that wasn't enough, she made the fettuccine Alfredo.

Over our pasta dishes and after a couple of glasses on wine, I told Lilly about the developments in Jamie's case. Like everyone else, she was shocked that a doctor would commit such an act. She wasn't shocked to learn about Jamie's sexuality.

"Will, I suspected Jamie might be gay. Not that it mattered to me. He never made a pass at me. As I told you, he was always a gentleman. The most affection I ever received was a peck on the cheek, and that was after three dates. He was a great guy, and I would have been happy to be his friend. But, I wouldn't have been happy to live a lie."

After dessert, we sat on her sofa and watched a movie, although I have no idea what it was called. My eyes were on Lilly. During a commercial, she turned and kissed me. It wasn't any peck on the lips. Hers was a real kiss. Then she surprised me and asked, "Will, are you a gentleman?"

I wasn't sure how to respond, so I decided to answer her with another question. "Do you want me to be?"

I'm not the kind of guy to kiss and tell. In that respect, I'm a gentleman. When I left Lilly's apartment on Sunday, I was walking on air. I promised to make her dinner at my place the following Saturday night after we played a round of golf. That week couldn't go fast enough for me.

34

File No. 16-12-07MCI

On my way home, I stopped by the office. About the last thing I wanted to do on a Sunday afternoon was work, but I had some things to finish with respect to Jamie McIntyre's case. My invoice to Mrs. McIntyre topped my list. It represented a large sum of money. I completed the invoice, attached a cover letter, and placed both in a business-sized envelope addressed to Mrs. McIntyre. If she received it by Tuesday or Wednesday, she might send me a check by the end of the week. I hoped to meet with her and wrap up all that was connected to this case.

Because I could expect to testify for the prosecution at Dr. Overstreet's trial, I had to organize all my reports, data, and discs together in a file. As I punched holes in reports, my telephone rang. Mike White was on the other end of the line.

"Will, I hoped I'd find you at your office today. Guess what? Overstreet took a plea. He accepted first degree manslaughter. No fuss, no muss. He'll spend a lot of time in jail for his crime."

"Great, Mike. Now, you tell me after I completed the file."

"Will, guess what else?"

"I have no idea, Mike. What?"

"I handed in my retirement papers. This case made me realize that it's time for me to turn in my badge. I let this one get away from me, and I let you down in the process"

"Jeez, Mike, don't be so hard on yourself. You were up against a savvy guy. Who would ever think a doctor from the medical examiner's office would try to pull off such a crime. In the end, you came through for me, and that's what counts." I meant what I said. Mike's friendship was more important to me than any case. So, I asked him, "Mike, what do you plan to do with your retirement?"

"Fish, and get under Tonya's feet." We laughed.

Then without hesitations, I said, "Mike, why don't you come in with me? My firm may not be glamorous, but it keeps me off the streets. I've got a lot of things in the hopper. You could bring some depth, bench strength, and a different approach."

"Yeah, I could balance your crazy onion approach with my tried and true orange approach. You know the one we were taught right out of the police academy by Sergeant Coughlin?"

"I remember, Mike. So what do you think?"

"What would we call our new firm, Orange and Onion?"

"No, smart ass. I think we should call it Prescott, White, and Associates. That has a nice ring to it. What do you think?"

"Sounds great to me if you're serious, Will."

"Mike, I couldn't be more serious. Why don't we meet Tuesday and discuss it at Alf's? You can buy me lunch."

Mike laughed. "Okay. I'll see you Tuesday at noon."

Even though Lilly served me a short stack of pancakes, four link sausages, and two fried eggs before she sent me on my way that morning, I was hungry. After I stopped by the post office to drop the envelope in the mailbox, I headed to McDonald's. I decided to try the chicken nuggets again. Maybe they tasted better hot. At the drive-through window, I picked up my order, which consisted of eight chicken nuggets, large fries, and large Diet Coke. Just in case the chicken nuggets didn't fill me, I asked the attendant to add a Big Mac.

I polished off my meal in about twenty minutes. It turned out I was hungrier than I thought. I was also more tired than I thought. I hit the hay at about eight that night and slept through until my alarm went off at seven the next morning. As soon as I shaved, showered, and dressed, I headed back to the office. I had to return Walter Thompson's call, and I wanted to call John MacKay at Gaming: The System and Sue Alsop at the security company to inform them about the arrest of Dr. Miles Overstreet. After those calls, I intended to meet with Monique Lewis before I met with Mike at Alf's Bar and Grill.

Walter Thompson asked to meet me on Wednesday morning at ten. He had two assignments for me. Mr. Thompson was shocked to learn that Jamie McIntyre was murdered and thanked me for my efforts to bring the case to a prompt resolution for Mrs. McIntyre.

Like Mr. Thompson, John MacKay expressed his appreciation for my work. John asked if I could help the company with some security issues. He promised to call me later in the week to set up a time for us to meet. Meanwhile, I suggested he contact Lieutenant Mike White about Jamie McIntyre's laptop. Because the police impounded Jamie's Lexus, it was off limits to me. If the laptop wasn't in the car, it was up to the police to search Dr. Overstreet's apartment and office for it.

When I reached Sue Alsop, I thanked her and explained the surveillance flash drive was the key to the resolution to the case. She was overjoyed to hear her firm helped to make a difference. I decided to take the plunge and try to set up an appointment to meet with her.

"Sue, perhaps we could get together for lunch, and you could tell me more about your firm and I could tell you about mine."

"Yes, Will. I'd like that. What about Thursday?"

"Great. Where will I meet you?"

"Why don't you stop by my office around eleven thirty. I'll show you around here first and then we can eat at the steakhouse across the street."

By ten, I was on my way to see Monique Lewis. She was a changed woman when she answered the door. Her smile lit up her face and she looked fifteen years younger.

"Will, I've made us a pot of coffee. And, I've set out some cookies, banana bread, and some of those raspberry tarts you like. I know it was difficult for you to say much when Lieutenant White was here. But he's not here now, so please tell me everything."

Monique sat on the edge of her seat while I spoke. She was fascinated. Despite the distress she experienced over the past six months, Monique was upbeat. When I told her the big white rabbit was Dr. Overstreet in his white biohazard coverall, she laughed and said, "So I wasn't crazy after all?"

"No, Monique. You weren't crazy nor were you responsible for Jamie McIntyre's death. However, I hope you don't mix alcohol and your medications in the future."

"Will, I promise to be careful, but as you know, I don't drive anymore, so it won't be an issue. Jason Slack has my car now. Wait until I tell him what's happened. But even if I did drive, I don't expect to come across a body in the middle of the road ever again."

"Well, Monique, if you do, call me. You've got my number."

Acknowledgments

While *Onions and Oranges* is a work of fiction, it takes place in a real city, Sacramento, California.

Real people also helped make this book possible. To them, I wish to express my gratitude, especially Edye Allen, Flore Baudouin, Dan Ernst, Jan Ernst, Bernadette Johannessen, Jo-Anne Robertson, Peter Robertson, and Steven Taylor. Their comments appeared on the back cover of a previous edition. For this edition, they appear below:

What a delightful and wonderful book! I want to read it all over again." —Edye Allen, Oregon

"Meticulously concocted. *Onions and Oranges* brings powerful and tangy flavors together, A piquant roller coaster ride." —Flore Baudouin, California

"If you like whodunnits, then you will love *Onions and Oranges*." —Dan Ernst, Florida

"I thoroughly enjoyed *Onions and Oranges*—finished the last 100 pages in one wonderful afternoon. I love Big Macs too!" —Jan Ernst, Florida

"*Onions and Oranges* kept me guessing. Kathy's style is unpretentious and straightforward. She's made a regular reader out of this non-reader."

—Bernadette Johannessen, Florida

"Like Kathy's other books, I enjoyed *Onions and Oranges*. Her writing style is impressive. Willis Prescott is so comfortable. It was like I was in the company of an old friend."

—Jo-Anne Robertson, Ontario, Canada

"*Onions and Oranges* has a nice cadence and well-developed characters. The outcome was not what I expected. And, as it turns out, oranges do have 10 segments—I checked."

—Steven Taylor, Connecticut

Also real are family and friends who inspire me to keep writing. My husband, Terry, is first among a great team of cheerleaders. Thank you all for your support.

About the Author

Kathy Dorsey lives in central Florida with her husband. They moved to Florida, in 2017, from California. Kathy was born in Toronto, Canada.

Onions and Oranges is Kathy's third of four books. Kathy's first book, *Just Jeeves: Life lessons from the end of a short leash* was published in 2019. *Just Jeeves* is a collection of her weekly columns that appeared in the *Lincoln News Messenger* and on her blog. Kathy's second book, *Sidewalk Spots*, was published in 2020. *Sidewalk Spots* is a quirky coming-of-age mystery that starts in San Francisco and winds up in a small northern California city called Gnome. *Onions and Oranges* is Kathy's first murder mystery. It takes place in Sacramento and features Private Investigator Willis Prescott. Kathy's fourth book, *Mary Ellen* was published n 2023. It takes up the story of the character, Mary Ellen, who was introduced in *Sidewalk Spots*. It's a touching and poignant novel that's been described as therapeutic.

To contact Kathy Dorsey, please email her at kdorseyucg@gmail.com.